1

I am homesick. I am always homesick. I will forever be homesick.

My mom seems to think that just because she has dragged me down to Doven, Florida that I would love it here with her as much as she loves to tan. And that's a lot of love. I hate the sun and she knows it, but she is very oblivious to my feelings.

My brother, Oliver, and I have always known she is quite selfish and never puts anyone before herself.

Oliver would test our theory when we were younger and living in Illinois. He would ask for lunch money and her response tended to be, "Oliver, you know I need the child support money to do my hair. I have lunch with a 'friend,' and I need to look my best."

My mom has no friends. In Washington, she had tons of friends. More than I could count. But as soon as the divorce papers were signed - thanks, dad - she has moved Oliver and I all around the country.

After Washington, it was Colorado; where she met a man and fell in love. But on the eve of her wedding, she was sent papers anonymously, of course, of his jail record. Let's just say, if each crime represented a person, then we would have our own little army. She ended up becoming the runaway bride and taking us off to Illinois. By this time, Oliver was entering high school and I was just about to enter sixth grade. In Illinois, mom got a job, finally, as a receptionist at Don's Car Lot where "he sells cars faster than you can say whoopee!" After about one week of work, she was sleeping with Don, a married man. His wife found out from her friend who walked in on him grabbing her butt. Don's wife found our address and inevitably egged our house and spray painted "home wrecker" on our lawn. I got up the next morning to get the paper and found the vandalism. Mom tried to tell me whoever did it must have the wrong house. The next day, mom was out of work, and we were on our way to West Virginia.

At first, we lived in Rambler, but Oliver got expelled from their high school for smoking in the bathroom, so we had to move. Mom said she didn't like the town anyways because the people looked at her weird. I didn't blame them.

My mom was petite with honey blonde hair to her waist, which she kept in curls everyday, and she had a Cindy Crawford mole. She tended to dress appropriately, but she still looked like a super model. She was always on me about staying in shape because her sister was fat, and she didn't want me to end up that way.

She would say to me every time I ate a piece of pizza or had some ice cream, "Scarlett, a moment on the lips, forever on the hips."

There was another thing about my mom that no one approved of; her age. She was only nineteen when she had

Oliver with my dad. She was going to school to be a nurse and he was a doctor right out of medical school.

He was about 26 when he met my mom.

I heard the story many times when I was younger.

"I was doing my charts for the night," my mom would take this time to pause to take a drink of water, "when I met him. I looked up from the chart I was doing, which I believe was for Charles Downer, who had just checked in that night with heart-burn." She would always think of new details every time she told the story. "And I saw this man just staring at me. The nurses were talking about him earlier, but I paid no attention to them because I had a job to do. Anyways, he was tall with a scruffy beard and dark brown hair that was curly, but very short. He had the greenest eyes I had ever seen. He walked over, and said, 'miss, I think that pencil has had enough torture for the night.' I was so confused, but then remembered, I had been chewing on a pencil, which now was about to snap in half. I laughed and that's when we began talking. After a couple of conversations, he asked me out on a date and then was propos-ing four dates later."

This was where she would start crying to amp up the story.

"Scarlett, I didn't even see it coming. One day I was engaged and in love. And the next, I was six days late and pee-ing on a stick. I don't regret having Oliver for a second, but I wish I had waited until after we were married."

And then by 22, she had two kids, no job, but a rich hus-band.

She inevitably relied on my dad for everything because she made no effort in trying to get a job. She also relied on our nanny, a small Spanish woman who never spoke, but loved to sing to Oliver and me at night, when mom was out and dad was working the night shift.

Anyways, after Rambler, we were off to Huntington, which was about 3 hours away from Rambler, so there was no chance in any of us seeing familiar people.

We stayed in Huntington until the end of my sophomore year of high school. Oliver was off in the Peace Corp; it was either that or the Army.

I had one friend in Huntington. In all of the places mom dragged me too, I tried to keep a low profile, knowing that I would be moving shortly.

But in Huntington, I decided to take a risk and meet Casey. Oliver was always adventurous, but I stuck with the rules of our houses - though there weren't many - I did the chores, and I cooked.

So Casey was my first risk, if you would call her that. She wasn't quiet, she was always in someone's pants and she was always at the best parties of the night. She was beautiful with her thick brown hair that she kept wavy and she had a very tall, lean body.

I went to a party that someone had I figured accidentally given me the information for. When I went that night, I realized I was a little out of my element. All of the girls around me were tall, skinny, and had shiny blonde hair. It looked like someone had gotten a hold of a clone machine and decided to produce the same girl 15 times. I, however, was tall with long mahogany brown hair that went to the middle of my back. I was not athletic looking, but not petite. I was skinny, but not too skinny. I definitely wasn't flat chested. Since no one ever noticed me, I was never made fun of for my boobs.

I had never had a boyfriend, and I wasn't holding my breath for one either.

I walked into the house, in which the party was being held in, and saw a girl wearing a tight black shirt with a plunging neck line even though she was very flat chested. She had too much eye liner on and her mascara was smeared. Her camo pants were clearly too big for her, but she seemed not aware of it.

She walked up to me and said very politely, "Move bitch."

I didn't hear her parting words, but I did smell beer mixed with vodka in her breath.

I turned around and then realized I had been in front of the bathroom.

The girl was vomiting what seemed everything her body contained into the toilet.

I didn't know what to do, but go and hold her hair.

My mom had her nights where she came home late from drinking the martinis or long island ice teas that were sent to her table from the guys at the bar that normally ranged from college guys all the way to middle aged men, looking for trophy wives.

The girl seemed about done after I had been holding her hair for five minutes.

I got a rag and wiped the eyeliner that had gotten smeared on her cheeks.

She smiled at me and then croaked, "I'm Casey and you're a lifesaver."

It was the first thing anyone had said to me that was remotely nice.

I blurted out, "It's no big deal, who hasn't had this problem, right?" Though, I had never had a drink in my life and didn't plan on drinking until I was of the legal age.

Casey smiled, but then looked past me because someone had called her name.

"Casey, there you are. I see we've had a bit too much tonight."

I turned around and saw a man that was probably about 50 or so, with dark gray hair and a scruffy beard. He didn't look like he was uncomfortable at the party though behind him a couple was making out in the corner.

"Hey dad," Casey began.

DAD?!? What was a dad doing at a party? Was this girl just normally a heavy drinker and her dad would come to pick her up after the throwing up was over?

"I drove here, so what should I do about my car?" Casey asked.

"I can take it," I said faster than I could realize what I was saying.

Both Casey and her dad looked at me awed. Her dad seemed surprised and I figured he didn't even know I was standing there in the first place; I usually had that effect on people. But Casey, she was just smiling at me while digging her keys out of her back pocket.

"Thanks again, lifesaver." She winked.

"No problem, I was thinking about leaving anyways."

Casey got up and both her dad and I followed her out of the bathroom to the main room of the house. As I walked, I glanced down at the set keys I had. A Mercedes? This should be fun driving.

We got out into the driveway and onto the street with silence.

I looked around for a beautiful, shiny Mercedes and then found it a few yards down the street.

"Look, be careful with my baby. I never let anyone drive it, but since you seem to be my own little lifesaver," she pinched my cheek, "I feel as if I owe you, so most people want to drive it, and here's your chance."

"I'm a great driver. No worries. I will just follow you guys back to your house."

"Wait, what about your car?" Casey asked.

I hadn't even given much thought to my own car when here someone was actually talking to me. What about my car? I bet I can get my mom to drive me to get it tomorrow, but on second thought...

"Oh, don't worry about it. I'll just have my mom's assistant come pick it up tomorrow," I lied.

If Casey knew I was lying, she wasn't showing it. "Oh okay. Well I'll just see you back at the house."

I watched her walk to her dad's Porsche while I walked to her gorgeous silver Mercedes. Was I really allowed to drive this? Or was it just a joke that I didn't get? Would she make me pay for damages if I accidentally hit a bird or got a bug on the spotless windshield?

I got into the car and waited for her dad to drive by me. When he drove by, Casey waved but seemed to be in the middle of a conversation. But it didn't look like her dad was mad at her or they were fighting. It looked as if she was telling him about how her day went. Is this really how her life is? If so, I wanted to be a part of it.

As we drove through Huntington, I looked at all the buildings that I wanted to become familiar with. I realized maybe this could be the place where I ended up finishing high school.

Once we got to her house, a mansion of course, I handed Casey her keys.

I don't think she ever knew this, but out of the corner of my eye I could tell she was giving her car a look over for any nicks or scratches.

"You really did me a huge favor by doing this," she said.

"You didn't ask, so it's not a favor. Don't worry about it," I said politely.

"Well anyways, I just wanted to say thanks again, lifesaver."

I smiled and walked away. My house was only about a mile from here. But suddenly I turned around.

"Hey Casey," she turned around at the call of her name, "its Scarlett by the way. My name I mean. It's Scarlett"

"Oh, right. Nice to meet you Scarlett," she said while smiling.

After that night, Casey and I gradually became best friends and I changed a lot. I drank all of the time, or at least when Casey drank, which is a lot, and I wore heavy eye liner. But that wasn't what made me different. People knew my name. I had boyfriends. I had friends.

Even though my mom wasn't happy about my transformation, I was.

I was with Casey all of the time and with her on and off again boyfriend, Demetri.

Demetri was the kind of guy who if you went to a college party, he was the first to hit on you. I never liked him or his sandy blonde hair that he wore short. Casey was in love with him though. He would cheat on her, she would break up with him, and then he would show up on her doorstep with a dozen roses begging for an apology. It happened so often that Casey and I had it down to a routine.

Someone would call Casey and tell her about Demetri cheating on her. Then she would call me, and I would stop whatever I was doing, or get up out of bed, and I would go to the gas station and get chocolate; any kind of chocolate. I would make my way towards her house and sit with her in bed talking about how stupid Demetri was.

This would go on for about 3 hours then she would fall asleep from crying and I would make my way towards Demetri's apartment. I remember the first time I went over there, Casey had no idea - she actually had no idea about all of the other times either - and if she ever asked about what I would do before her waking up after crying I would tell her I went home and got cleaned up, which I actually did before I went to Demetri's.

The first time went a little like this...

I knocked on his door and waited for him to answer.

"Scarlett," he said after opening the door, "how's Case doin'?"

"I don't know Demetri; you cheated on her with some blonde bimbo at a college party, so why don't you tell me?"

"Look Scarlett, I get your mad, but this is between Case and me, which brings me to my question, why are you here?"

I didn't know why I was here. To tell him off? To beat him up? He was big, but I figured I could take him.

"Uh, I just wanted to tell you that you need to apologize to her and try to make up."

"Why would I do that? I can get ass from anyone of the girls at the high school or even at the junior college. So Scarlett, please tell me why I should go crawling back to Casey when she is not even the one I like?"

What was he talking about? This is why I hated him. He never even liked her and he had just admitted to it. So why was he dating her then? He just said he doesn't have to date her in order to have sex.

"What do you mean she is not the one you like?" I questioned.

It took him a few minutes to respond. I was about to ask him again but then he answered my question.

"Scarlett, are you blind? Casey is so trashy, and you are so classy. I like you Scarlett, not Casey. The night I went up to you guys at the party, I was going to ask you out, not her. I felt sorry for her, that's why I didn't push it. But now since her and I are over, why don't we give it a go?" He said, while winking at me.

"Are you kidding me? You just broke up with my best friend and now you're asking me out? And why would I date you when you just admitted you can 'get ass from all the girls at the high school and the junior college'? I mean seriously Demetri, you are amazingly stupid," I yelled.

"I'm going to act like you didn't say that Scarlett because I know you like me and I definitely like you so why don't you just come in and we'll talk about this?"

I knew if I went into his apartment Casey and I would never be friends again, once she found out. But yet, I still went in without a moment's hesitation.

After that, every time Casey and Demetri broke up - I convinced him if he kept dating her that she wouldn't ever suspect Demetri and me sleeping together whenever we had the chance – I was there for her, even though she deserved way better.

But then one day, Demetri and I slipped up and Casey found us in his bed.

Let's just say, she called me a few names that would never be allowed on national television. Even though she found us, she stayed with Demetri. Demetri kept calling me, telling me that we would just have to be more careful. And truthfully, I wanted more than anything to be with him because he made me feel beautiful and always told me that he loved me even though I knew it was a ploy.

The news was all over town and my mom heard two women talking about it at the nail salon. She came home and sat me down and asked me if I wanted to move.

"But mom, aren't you mad at me? I mean I committed adultery, so shouldn't I get punished or something?"

"Sweetie, you loved him and that's okay. I've been there before, when I was younger of course - she still hadn't figured out that I knew about her and Don - and it will get worse if we don't move. You'll be called names constantly and you probably won't have any friends."

This was my mom being nice. But everything she was saying was true. I declined the offer and went back to school where I was called many names and had no friends. It was almost like my first day, but on my first day, no one called me a slut.

After about a week of this, I sat down with my mom and told her that she was right and we needed a new start. I had just finished my sophomore year and I was ready for something innovative. Oliver was gone and it was just mom and I on the open road.

And now, here we are in Doven, Florida where I'm about to begin another life.

2

Over the summer I stopped wearing make up on the request of my mother, but I didn't oppose because I knew that wearing heavy make up and being skanky wasn't me.

On the last night in Huntington, mom came into my room with a bottle of beer and said, "Drink this and enjoy it because it's the last drink you'll be having for a long time." I didn't know if it was a trick or something so I eyed the bottle, but didn't pick it up. She said, "if you don't drink it then you'll never feel satisfied and plus, I'm not leaving until you drink it and that's a promise."

I picked up the bottle and chugged the beer. It burned my throat, but I didn't want to get into trouble. Feeling satisfied, my mom left the room to let me enjoy my mini buzz.

After that night, my mom and I never talked about my drinking or having sex with my best friend's boyfriend.

Once we got to Doven, we moved into a small house that was yellow with blue shutters. It had two bedrooms which were basically telling my brother "you're not welcome here." I wanted him back, but I knew him and mom got into a big fight before we left Huntington. Even though he wasn't living with us, he told mom that she needs to stop lugging me around and that I need to have a normal life. He had called her late at night in the hopes that I was sleeping.

When she hung up and went to bed, I went downstairs and called him and told him about how I was drinking and how Casey - whom he had never met - walked in on me and Demetri. I didn't feel uncomfortable talking about it to him because Oliver and I were really close and plus I knew about all of the times he slept with his best friends' girlfriends.

Oliver told me to tell my mom sorry and that he overreacted, but I never did. Oliver was my brother and I didn't want him getting close to mom because I knew if they got close then he would take her away from me right when we are starting to get along.

So in her mind, she and Oliver were fighting and that he had no idea what he was talking about.

* * *

On the morning of my first day at Doven High, I wasn't like any other teenage girl trying to dress to impress. I slipped on a pair of jeans and a blue t-shirt. I knew I was going to get hot in jeans, but I was trying to give my mom a message that when I said I wanted to leave, I meant I wanted to go somewhere were rain was constant, not where it's sunny every day.

Ever since I was young, I had always hated the sun. I would get burnt easily and then instead of the burn turning into a tan, I would immediately go straight back to being very pale. My mom always said being pale fit with my blue eyes so I had no worries, even though I was never worried.

The truth was I wanted to go back to Washington to see my dad. He never called, but I knew that was only because of how he ended things with mom. I was homesick for my real home even though mom considered every new town our home. I never bought it.

As I made my way to the kitchen I noticed something on the table. Breakfast? No, it couldn't be. My mom didn't know how to cook and she would never make the gesture that she knew how to because she liked how I cooked while she did "her chores" (tanning, hair, nails).

There was no breakfast on the table, but a note.

Scarlett,

I'm going on a job hunt today. Last night I had an epiphany and I realized its time! So good luck at school today and I'll be home at 5 expecting dinner!

Love,
Mom

Since when did it take ten hours to find a job?

While my mind raced with possibilities, I got out a bowl, spoon, milk, and cereal.

This would be my amazing breakfast for my new start.

Why would she want a job? I had always thought job was a three letter word to her and that poor people were the only ones who really needed one. Did she even know what an epiphany was and how did she even know how to spell it? Apparently, I wasn't giving her enough credit. Could she possibly have a new boyfriend and she wanted to spend all day with him? If she was getting a new job, let's hope for a woman as a boss.

Once I was finished I put the bowl and spoon in the sink; I guess I'll be doing the dishes later. I was out the door to my Ford Focus in a speed that could be beaten by a turtle. I was in no hurry to start school. Weren't parents supposed to go with you on the first day to get you all set up? My mom didn't even call to tell them I was coming. I had to call myself and meet with the principal and everything.

At school, I parked in the farthest spot so I had enough time to kill.

The office was really cold; I guess it's better than the sweltering heat outside.

The woman behind the desk seemed to be about sixty. She had her gray hair thrown up in a bun on the top of her head. Her mascara was smeared, but not noticeably.

"Hi, I'm Scarlett Finely." The woman looked up and seemed like she didn't understand what I was saying. "I'm the new student. I came in about a week ago and met with Mr. Morris," I continued.

"Oh yes, that's right," the elderly woman said, "I'm Mrs. Moore. It's nice to meet you. I have your schedule right here." She handed me a bright orange paper with all of my classes on it. I looked down at it and saw that I had Algebra II first hour; great, that's the subject I'm worst at.

"Thanks, but can you give me directions to the some of the classes? Mr. Morris only showed me a few rooms," I confessed.

The woman seemed pleased for no reason I could think of. "Well of course. I can show you them right now. We'll end on your first class so you won't be late." She smiled.

"Thanks that would be great."

As we walked through the school and Mrs. Moore pointed to classes, I couldn't help but notice the glances I was getting. Normally on my first day, no one would even give me a second look. But here, everyone was looking at me; guys, girls, and teachers.

I nodded every time Mrs. Moore said something, trying to look interested.

"And here we are. This is Mr. Rainer's class. School is about to start so come to the office at lunch and if you have any questions you can ask them then. By the way, your locker is right there," she said while pointing to a locker no more than five feet away from me.

"And here is your locker combination." She pointed to the orange paper where my locker number and combination was.

"Alright, thank you," I said politely.

"Well, you are certainly welcome." She seemed taken back by my politeness. Teachers at all of the schools were never taken back by it, but were appreciative.

I walked into the class with my book bag over one shoulder.

I approached the teachers desk where - Mr. Rainer? - was standing shuffling papers.

Before I spoke, I looked at the audience I had. What was with this school? Everyone was just staring at me.

"Hi, I'm Scarlett Finely."

Mr. Rainer looked up and nodded while handing me a book. "Yes, hello. I'm Mr. Rainer. It's nice to meet you Scarlett. Would you like to introduce yourself or should I?"

What? Please no introductions. Teachers never did this to me.

"Um, you can. But is it okay if I take a seat?"

He seemed to not understand, but nodded anyways.

I didn't want to stand for this so he pointed to an empty desk and I quickly walked to it.

The bell was going to ring at any moment and he was going to introduce me. Should I just smile? Or should I say hi? Or could I just stare at the desk and hope for it to end soon? I liked the last option the most.

But when I sat down, I noticed everyone wasn't looking at me. I'm glad I'm not interesting anymore.

I looked out of the corner of my eye and saw someone staring very intensely at me. I turned my whole head to look at him or her.

He was really good looking, but not in an obvious way. He didn't remind me of Demetri at all. He had dark brown hair with brown eyes and a striking jaw line. He was definitely good looking enough to be a model, but not a pretty boy model. I couldn't really explain it.

At Huntington after I met Casey, I became more confident, so if I were still there, I would have winked at the amazing guy, but instead I could feel myself blushing, so I immediately looked away.

The loud bell rang.

"Class, this is Scarlett Finely." Mr. Rainer did a Vana White style gesture towards me.

All the students turned to look at me. Yikes, I had their attention again.

I looked up and smiled, but then went back to staring at my desk.

"Scarlett, why don't you tell us where you're from," Mr. Rainer said.

He was going to be the death of me.

I hesitated for a minute. Everyone in their seat waited patiently for me to say something.

"I'm from West Virginia." That was all I was going to give them. There was no way for them to hear about the whole thing in Huntington, but I wasn't going to take any chances.

"Oh, that's nice. Where in West Virginia?" Mr. Rainer pressed.

"Uh, Huntington. It's really small. I think the population is about six hundred people." What was I doing? I could have just said Rambler, but what if someone found out I had lived in Huntington after Rambler? I was talking too much already. This is where it would end.

"That is very small indeed." He smiled.

Alright, I think it was over. If every teacher makes me do this I will make my story short and simple.

All of the students turned back in their seats, but the guy sitting next to me was still staring at me.

The whole hour was boring and I wasn't even listening. I was definitely going to fail this class, but mom never cared about grades.

When the hour was over I decided to go to my locker to put my new Algebra II book in it. I went to locker 345 and while I was in the process of putting in the combination I saw someone just standing next to me. What if it was that guy? I don't know what I would say.

But when I looked, it wasn't a guy at all. It was a girl that I think was in Algebra II with me. She had short hair that was bright red with pretty curls in it. Her eyes were brilliant green and she was smiling at me.

"Hi, Scarlett, I'm Elaine. I was in your Algebra II class last hour," she confirmed my suspicions. Her southern accent was so thick I couldn't help, but think about it.

"Hi Elaine," I said. I was trying to give off the impression that what just happened last hour was not me at all because I never spoke.

"So Scarlett, I know first days can be tough. I moved here three years ago from Houston. If you want to sit by me at lunch, you can. I would love to know more about you." Why was she being overly nice? It was very creepy and I had the sudden urge to walk away. But I didn't want to come off mean to anyone that was being really nice to me, so I fought the urge.

"Actually, Mrs. Moore said I need to come into the office today at lunch. But is it okay if I sit by you tomorrow?" I needed somewhere to sit. At all the other schools I would eat in the library, but I have yet to find the library.

"Oh, that would be great. But beware of Mrs. Moore. Once she has you on her hook she won't let you go. When I came here she asked me to come in at lunch and then kept asking me to come in everyday for no reason. It was really creepy."

"Oh okay," I laughed.

"So what do you have this next hour?" Elaine asked.

I looked down at my schedule.

"I have Junior English with Mrs. Eisner. Is that how you pronounce it?"

"Yeah. Last year when I had her I would pronounce it wrong and she would correct me every time. Anyways, good luck with that class. And I really mean it. No one passes with an A."

I wasn't going to doubt her on that.

"How about you? What do you have next hour?" I asked.

"Senior English."

"Oh, you're a senior?"

"Yeah, I'm taking Algebra II this year because I failed it last year. I tell ya, I'm terrible at that subject."

I laughed. "Probably not as bad as me."

She smiled. "Well, it was nice to meet you. I'll see you tomorrow for more math time!"

"Definitely," I said with a sarcastic smile.

It was really odd how nice she was. Did she know something about me that I didn't want her to know? But how would she or anyone else in this school find out?

As I made my way towards Junior English with Mrs. Eisner, I couldn't help but notice everyone was still looking at me. Did I have something in my teeth? But I wasn't smiling so there was no way they could know that there was something in my teeth. Was there something wrong with my outfit? That couldn't be it because almost everyone here was just wearing jean shorts and shirts.

Maybe that was it. Because I was wearing jeans. Hasn't someone come to school with jeans on here?

I saw that my class was less than four feet from me now.

Behind her desk- Mrs. Eisner I guessed- was talking to the class.

I walked into the room and saw everyone was staring at me just like an hour ago.

I approached the desk, "Hi, I'm Scarlett Finely." I smiled at this very old woman that really needed to retire and it looked like she was hoping to soon.

"Here is your book," she handed me the textbook, "and you can have a seat there." She pointed to the desk in the very front. Why did this woman hate me so much? At least Mr. Rainer let me sit in the back, but here in the front, I would be able to feel all of the eyes daggering at me.

"Um, thanks." I walked slowly to the empty desk.

"By the way, 'um' is not a word. I have to give you props for using it in front of the English teacher," Mrs. Eisner was saying. She clearly didn't like me.

"I'm sorry," I apologized.

Everyone was trying to fight back their laughs.

As I sat down in my chair, I noticed a guy wink at me. Why did he just wink at me?

He looked vaguely familiar and I couldn't realize why.

That would be my mission the whole class instead of listening to Mrs. Eisner and she didn't seem to mind me not speaking again.

The guy had sandy blonde hair and smiled at me when I turned around to get a glance at him. He had very charming dimples. He sort of looked like Demetri.

He was really cute though, so if he wanted to wink at me, I guess that would be okay.

During the whole hour Mrs. Eisner talked about our syllabus that she had passed around. She paused about every minute to take a drink of her coffee. There was no way there was any coffee left by the end of the hour.

When the bell rang, I tried to get out of there as fast as I could.

I heard loud foot steps behind me.

I turned around to see who was following me.

It was the guy with the sandy blonde hair.

"Hey, I'm Chase. I was in your Junior English last hour?" He said it like a question. "Anyways, I just wanted to introduce myself."

"Um, hi, I'm Scarlett," I said.

"Don't you remember that 'um' isn't a word?" He winked.

"Oh yeah. I mean yes, sorry."

"Its cool, I was just kidding around Scarlett," he said my name like he knew me, "but Mrs. Eisner is tough. I was going to say hi, but she started class too soon."

"Yeah, I couldn't help but notice you wink at me." I didn't like this guy. He gave me the creeps so I might as well make him feel uncomfortable.

"Well I couldn't help but notice you." He smiled.

"Thanks, I guess."

"Anytime. And I mean that, anytime. I was thinking that after lunch we could hang out."

"Thanks, but no thanks. I already have plans and I don't even know you," I said rudely.

He was taken back by this. You could tell he wasn't used to getting rejected.

"Oh okay, well maybe tomorrow."

Was he not getting that I didn't want to hang out with him, which probably meant making out with him behind the dumpster or something.

"I have plans tomorrow too," I remembered Elaine's offer.

"Look Scarlett, I like you even though I just met you. But I really want to talk to you because I think you might want to hear what I have to say," he said with a smile.

"Look Chase, I don't think I want to hear what you have to say. Sorry, okay?"

I started to walk away. This guy was starting to get on my nerves.

"Wow, I bet you weren't this mean to Demetri!" he shouted at my back.

I paused. How did he know about Demetri? We were about one hundred and seventy five miles away from Huntington, so how did he know about him?

"What do you mean? How do you know Demetri?" I asked.

"Demetri Raider is my cousin, who just happens to visit me every summer. When he came down this summer, he told me all about a girl named Scarlett that had long brown hair and a nice rack. He said she was beautiful. Once I saw you, I knew you were the Scarlett Demetri was talking about. He said you guys had a relationship and that he was finally falling for you when his girlfriend who I think was your best friend," he smiled because he knew this was agony for me, "found you in his bed. Nice by the way. Very classy."

Classy. Was. The. Word. Demetri. Used. That was when I knew this life was over for me.

"Um, I have no idea what you are talking about. I was friends with Demetri last year, but that was it. We were just friends and nothing more," I said very fast. I had to try to recover from this.

"Yeah, friends with benefits. Anyways, I was just hoping maybe since Demetri was my cousin you could help me out. You know friends with benefits?"

"Why would I do that?" I asked.

"Well, since you're new, you have a rep to protect. I don't think you'll be too popular with people knowing your past. No girl would trust you around their boyfriends. But me, I'm single. We wouldn't have to tell anyone anything."

"Why are you doing this to me? Can't we just drop it?"

"No, but I will see you after lunch today," he said with a smile.

"But I told you have plans. I really do have plans today."

"Yeah, Elaine told me you had to have lunch with Mrs. Moore. Just blow her off. She has probably forgotten about it already. And plus if you don't meet me behind the school today at lunch, you'll regret it."

I was too preoccupied to hear his threat. "Wait, why did Elaine tell you that? Are you friends with her?"

"Elaine is my best friend's girlfriend. So I bet your first friend here wouldn't let you sit with her if she knows about your past and believe me, I'm sure of it."

I was silent. Why was this kid doing this to me? Couldn't he just find some other girl to sleep with? He was definitely attractive enough. And why was I fighting this, he was cute. Chase was waiting for me to say something because I sucked in some air.

"So..?" he asked. "Do we have a deal?"

A deal? Is that what he thought of this as? I sleep with him and he doesn't ruin my life? Interesting deal, but I wasn't sure if I could handle it. And we were going to have sex behind the building at lunch? Wow, very classy.

"What time do you want me there?"

25

3

All of the classes before lunch were pretty uneventful. Most of the teachers let me introduce myself and didn't press after that. But everyone kept staring at me! I kept telling myself I was paranoid or if they were staring at me it was because of the jeans.

At lunch time, I didn't know what to do.

One option was to go to Mrs. Moore's office and enjoy a nice lunch with an elderly woman while knowing Chase was telling everyone about my past.

But option number two was to just blow off Mrs. Moore and try to apologize later. And I would go see Chase and do what he wanted me to do while thinking it would be over soon while I was doing it.

When I went to the spot Chase told me to meet him at – behind the library, which was outside, odd- and wait for him. He wasn't there, so I had time to prepare mentally.

I sat down on the ground with my head between my knees hoping this was all just a nightmare that I would wake up from at any time.

"There you are beautiful!" Chase yelled with a smiled.

"You told me to be here, so here I am." I said I would do this, but not nicely.

I stood up while he was walking towards me.

"Touchy, touchy. So do you understand what I want? We are friends with benefits. And I do mean friends. We can hang out as much as you want. Hell, if you want to call me your boyfriend, I wouldn't oppose." He winked at me.

"Yeah, sorry, I'll try to be nicer while you're blackmailing me. So how should we do this?" I asked.

"Uh, well I figured you would be a pro," he saw my grimace so he tried to recover. "I'm just kidding Scarlett. That's the way I am. I'll try to be nicer, sorry. By the way, I really do love your name. You never hear names like that these days."

Was he really trying to compliment me?

"Uh, thanks. So really, how do you want to do this I mean-"

Before I could finish my sentence he had my face in his hands and his lips were urgent against mine. He moved one hand to the small of my back and pressed me against him. His other hand was in my hair.

I didn't know what to do with me hands, so I put them in his hair.

He was surprisingly a good kisser.

He stopped the kiss to catch his breath.

"I knew you would like me," he said confidently.

"No, you're just a good kisser." I laughed.

"You may not like me now Scarlett Finely, but one day you'll open your eyes and see that I'm the one for you."

"Chase, you seem like a nice guy, so why blackmail me? I mean if you would have just asked me out and not even let me know you knew about my past, I would have said yes."

"I doubt that."

"I'm serious Chase," I said. Was I really admitting this all to him?

"Well, thanks." That was all he said before he had me in his grasp again.

I think I could really get used to this. Maybe he was right; I would end up falling for him.

All of a sudden I heard someone clear their throat.

Chase didn't hear them, or he didn't show that he heard them because he continued with our kiss. I grabbed his head and yanked him away, but grabbed his hand so he knew I wasn't ready to back out of the deal.

He smiled at me and then winked. He turned his head to see who the intruder was.

"Oh, hey Adam," Chase looked relieved, "what's up?"

I turned to see who Adam was and saw the guy that was staring at me in Algebra II.

"Chase," Adam had a very deep, calming voice, "I see you've met the new girl."

Was he talking about me? I heard Mr. Rainer introduce me so why didn't he just use my name?

"Her name is Scarlett," Chase said. It sounded like he was offended that Adam called me 'the new girl.'

"Oh yes, that's right, Scarlett." Adam eyed me, but returned his gaze to Chase.

"So, did you need something Adam?" Chase asked.

"No. I was coming from the library and I heard people talking and I was just seeing who it was, that's all." Adam sounded like he was being accused of something and that he needed to clear up the matter.

"Oh okay. So Adam would you like to introduce yourself?" Chase asked. I looked at him and he smiled and winked.

"Sure, I guess. Hey Scarlett, I'm Adam," he turned to look at me, "You seem to have met my younger brother, Chase."

YOUNGER BROTHER?!? That means Adam probably knew about Demetri and me. Could this day get any worse?

"Oh, it's nice to meet you, Adam. Yeah, Chase has Junior English with me."

"Oh, I see." Adam was clearly judging me, but he wasn't showing it in his eyes.

"Alright, now that the introductions are over, Adam do you mind?" Chase said.

"I'll just leave you two alone. Chase," he nodded to Chase, "Scarlett," he locked eyes with me for a second, but then looked away.

I watched him walk back from where he came from. He didn't look back once.

Once he was gone, I knew it was safe to talk.

"So, that was your brother?" I asked.

"Yeah, he is nothing like me and tends to creep people out." He laughed. "Though, he seemed to like you."

"What? He liked me? He didn't show it. He is in my Algebra II class and just stared at me the whole time. I think I know what you were talking about when you said he creeps people out."

"Hey, that is my brother you're talking about," Chase said with a chuckle.

"Sorry, I didn't mean offense. It was just...weird. That's all."

"No, it's cool. He and I never got along."

I didn't have time to get another word in because once again Chase had me in his grasp. We were back behind the library for another good fifteen minutes when the bell rang.

"Well, I guess I'll see you tomorrow, Scarlett?" Chase asked.

"Yeah, I'll be here, no worries." I smiled.

Chase laughed and then walked away so I could gather myself.

Why did he need to blackmail me in order to get a girl to kiss him? He had charm so I couldn't understand what his big mystery was that could repel him to girls.

* * *

When I got to my last class, I was tired and I just wanted to go back 'home.'

At least my last hour was easy; history. I had always liked history and history always liked me. At my last schools I had the best grades in this subject.

The teacher was a man that was short enough to be an elf, but he was very thin. His dark brown hair was beginning to fall out and his little beard was stringy. He seemed odd and his first words confirmed my suspicions of him.

"Ah, my gentle lady Scarlett Finely. How art thou?" His voice was normal, but went up in pitch at the end.

"I'm good, thanks. Where would you like me to sit?" I just wanted this to be over with.

"Well in the back is fine. And here is your textbook. Do you like Doven High so far?"

"Yeah, it's great."

"Oh yes, I forgot. I'm Mr. Tilden," he held out his hand, "it's nice to meet you."

None of the teachers had gestured their hand to me, so I was sort of taken back by it.

"It's nice to meet you too," I said while shaking his hand.

I walked to the back where there was an empty desk.

I looked around and some of the kids in the class looked familiar.

I looked to my left where there was a window showing the parking lot. And then to my right was Adam.

Adam? If Chase was a junior, then Adam must be a senior. But he is taking a lot of junior classes, interesting.

Adam met my gaze but didn't smile or wave. But since I was stupid, I smiled at him. He looked at me bored, but then his face flushed.

Did I just make him blush? Realizing that I did, I blushed too and looked away.

The bell rang, so last hour was finally beginning.

"Class, most of you probably have met Ms. Finely, but I figured I would introduce her anyways," Mr. Tilden said.

Everyone became silent and met Mr. Tilden's gaze towards me.

"So Ms. Finely would you like to introduce yourself?"

"Uh, sure. Hi, I'm Scarlett Finely." I was finally getting used this whole introduction thing.

Everyone stared at me, but I noticed Adam smiling.

"Alright, let's start class. I have your syllabus for this semester…"

Everyone turned around to listen to Mr. Tilden, but I turned my head to the left so I could stare out to the parking lot. I noticed something move. At the corner of the parking lot I saw red. It was Elaine getting into what I assumed was her car. She got in and checked herself in the mirror. She put the car in reverse and almost hit another car; clearly not the best driver. She stopped and put the car in drive and drove forward. I noticed her make up was all smeared. Had she been crying?

I heard someone clear their throat and turned my head to Adam, but he wasn't the one who had cleared their throat. Mr. Tilden was staring at me waiting for me to answer a question, I think.

"So, Ms. Finely, does that sound okay?" I looked around the class and saw everyone was staring at me once again.

"Uh, yeah. That sounds great." Hopefully I didn't just tell the teacher that giving me a detention sounded like a great idea.

"Alright, good. I'm glad you think a partner project is a great idea." He smiled and seemed pleased.

"So class, shall I pick the pairings?"

No one said anything.

"Alright, I'll take that as a yes because clearly you are all listening to me. So you and you," he pointed to two girls in the front, "are one pair and you and you are another." He went through all the rows then finally ended on me.

"And you Ms. Scarlett Finely will be partners with Mr. Adam Wilson. He is a great guy, I'm sure you'll do great work together."

I turned to look at Adam, but he was looking down at his desk. I couldn't tell what his facial expression was.

I looked away. Why did I have to be partners with this guy? I would prefer to have Chase right about now. Adam clearly didn't like me and I don't know where Chase got the idea that he did.

"The bell is about to ring, so tomorrow we'll assign topics. Have a nice day." Mr. Tilden finished with a smile.

The bell rang and I tried to gather my stuff as fast as I could.

Once I got to my locker I put everything in there because I had no homework for the night.

I went down the hall like a lightning bolt; nothing like how I had walked the hall this morning. I went to my car, but found a note on the windshield.

Scarlett,

I enjoyed today and I hope you did too. I look forward to seeing you tomorrow. And try to wear jean shorts to fit in!

Chase

Well, at least he was cute.

I got into my car, starting it and then turning the air conditioner up on high.

I might be able to get used to the heat, but I don't think I'll be able to get used to the people here.

I drove out of the parking lot as fast as I could; I didn't want to deal with these people any longer.

And now, I had to go home and deal with my biggest problem, my mom.

Out of all of the places I've been, I definitely hated Doven the most.

* * *

I drove home as fast as I could; I needed to prepare dinner.

Since I cook all the time, I've become quite the chef. Tonight I figured I would make steaks and baked potatoes.

My mom tried to watch what she ate, but she couldn't refuse a bake potato.

I turned on the oven and began to prepare the steak.

While I marinated the steak I went through the day again...

Why was Elaine being so nice to me? She would have never been nice to me if she knew my past, so she must not know, yet.

Was I falling for Chase even though he was blackmailing me? He must have a dirty little secret because he was so cute and charming; he should have already had a girlfriend.

And what was up with that Adam kid? Chase said he liked me, but I couldn't see it. And then he blushed when I smiled at him. Maybe he did like me, but what could I do about it when I have to make out with his brother everyday behind the library?

I looked down and the steak was covered with spices. Well, I guess that's mine.

I heard the keys in the door.

"Scarlett! Scarlett! My baby Scarlett!" my mom said while making her way towards the kitchen. "Guess what?"

"I don't know mom. Maybe you got a job?"

"Oh, no, but I did find a man!" she said with a wide grin.

"Mom, how did you already find a man? We've been here for less than two weeks."

She put her purse down, walked over to me, and put her hands on my shoulders.

"Sweetie, I actually met him over the internet when we were in Huntington. That's why I took us here; you're momma found her a man!"

"So you didn't want to move for me, but for yourself? Surprising."

"Hey kid, cut the 'tud. I don't know why you and Oliver," I winced at the name, "can't just realize that it's a tough life and I'm not being selfish, I just want to find someone."

"Oh really, it's a tough life for you?" I was saying so much. I had never told my mom how I really felt about her selfishness, but I figured why not ruin it?

My mom dropped her hands from my shoulders, surprised, I assumed.

"Because I'm the one who cooks, cleans, and does the shopping. For god's sake mom, I even pay the bills!" I shouted.

My mom looked like she was going to burst into tears at any moment.

"Well, then, I guess I now know how you really feel about the arrangement. I always thought you liked it," she blubbered.

She ran to her room and slammed the door shut.

Well, I guess I've ruined everything for myself here in Doven.

4

My mom didn't come out of her room that night. I threw both of the steaks away because I had lost my appetite. What was up with me and hurting people I loved?

First Casey and now my mom.

I just knew I would be making apologies later to my mom, so I went to my room.

But I didn't really want to apologize because I'm glad she knew about how I felt about our "arrangement." She liked it because her duty was nothing, but I had all the work on my back.

I sat on my bed and stared at the walls that were empty; I tried not to decorate them because I knew we would be leaving at an unexpected time, like always.

What about this new guy that my mom called her 'man'? Was he married too, or was he divorced? I really doubted he was her age. My mom was young and beautiful, but she had her thing for older guys.

Was I going to have to meet him? What about dad? When mom was about to get married in Colorado, dad went crazy.

I ended up falling asleep thinking about all the crazy information I had just learned.

* * *

When I got to school the next day, Elaine was at my locker.

"Hey Elaine, what's up?" I asked. I remembered seeing her leaving the parking lot crying yesterday.

"Hey, Scarlett. Oh nothing, except my boyfriend broke up with me yesterday." I froze. Did Chase lie to me and he was really the one dating her?

"Oh yeah? That sucks," I said nonchalantly.

"Yeah and then he has the nerve to tell me that he thinks it's for the best. Can you believe that?" Her southern accent got thicker and thicker with every word.

"That's crazy. Who was your boyfriend?" I winced waiting for the answer.

"Adam Wilson. I saw you talking to Chase, his brother yesterday. Did he say anything?"

Adam was her boyfriend? That's interesting.

Elaine was still waiting for an answer.

"Oh, no. Chase was just introducing his self to me yesterday. That was all."

"He is a great guy, isn't he? Way happier than Adam."

"Yeah, he seemed nice." If she was trying to trick me into saying something, I wasn't going to let it work.

The bell rang at that moment; thank God.

"Alright, I'll see you in like a minute," Elaine said with a laugh.

"Yeah, math time!" I said remembering her words yesterday.

She smiled and then walked towards Mr. Rainer's class.

So Adam was the one who broke up with her. He must have been able to see her in the parking lot yesterday. Is that why he blushed? He was embarrassed that someone had seen the evidence?

I walked into Algebra II with no eyes on me expect one pair – Adam's.

Why does he always stare at me? I had never gotten a guy's attention like I have here. I was ignored at all of my other schools; except Huntington, but that was only because I was best friends with the Casey, the school slut.

I sat down and stared at the dry erase board; I could still feel his eyes on me.

I turned my head slightly to catch a peek at his gorgeous face. When I looked at him though, he turned his head to stare at the front. Had he not realized I knew he'd been staring at me this whole time?

Mr. Rainer clapped his hands when the final bell rang.

"Class! Welcome," he turned his head to look in my direction, "and I see Scarlett, that we haven't scared you off yet," he said with a smile and then a wink.

More winking? What was with this school?

But no one was staring at me anymore. I must not be that interesting, or I was just very paranoid yesterday. I looked at Adam again, but this time he didn't turn his head.

We just sat there, with locked eyes the whole hour. He never looked away once and neither did I; who ever looked away first was the loser and I wasn't going to lose to Chase's brother.

I heard a pinging noise and realized it was the bell. But Adam still didn't leave his gaze to get his stuff.

I looked away; I couldn't handle it. I pondered the thought of asking Mr. Rainer for a new spot and when he asks why I'll just say the draft is terrible.

I got up and walked out of the class to see Elaine, once again at my locker. But she didn't look sad. Instead, she looked mad.

She must have seen Adam staring at me the whole hour.

I approached my locker with caution.

"Hey Elaine, boring class, right?" I needed to give the impression that there was nothing going on between Adam and me.

"I don't know, Scarlett," she said my name with disgust, "why don't you tell me?"

I opened my locker to get my English book out.

"Uh, yeah, it was very boring. I've always hated math," I said trying to sound oblivious.

"Scarlett, I saw Adam staring at you at the beginning of class, so please tell me what the hell is going on."

So she didn't see me staring at him. That was good. It made me look like the good guy; I knew I could get out of this now.

"Elaine, I have no idea why he was staring at me. It kind of creeped me out, to be honest," I said with a laugh.

She looked calmer now. "Oh, so there isn't anything going on with you guys?"

"No. Not at all. And I'm sorry if I gave the impression that there was something going on." I was clearly almost out of this.

"Oh okay. I'm really sorry Scarlett. I just saw how he was staring at you. I jumped to conclusions. Anyways, I'll see you at lunch?"

"Yeah, I might be a little late, but I'll definitely be there." I'll just try to cut my meeting with Chase a little short, even though, a little part of me didn't want too.

"Alright, so see you later," she said with a smile.

"Alright." I smiled.

Now I had to go to English and see Chase. Maybe this day will get better.

When I walked into class I saw Chase; he was the only one looking at me.

I must have been very paranoid yesterday because no one is staring at me. Or is it because I took Chase's advice and wore jean shorts and a purple v-neck shirt instead of jeans?

I walked to my desk and looked at Chase who was smiling at me. I returned the smile; he was too cute not to be nice too.

I sat down and waited for this boring class to be over.

Mrs. Eisner walked in at that moment with her mug of coffee; the coffee would be all gone by the end of the period, no doubt about it.

"Good morning class," Mrs. Eisner began, "let's begin, shall we?"

We all turned to page 19 in our textbooks after we were instructed to. She talked very slow, but very precisely. It made you want to go to sleep; I could tell what Elaine meant by no one passing the class with an A. It was probably because they were all asleep for Mrs. Eisner's lectures.

The whole hour was Mrs. Eisner talking about page 19. When the bell finally rang, I got my stuff and got up.

I felt a hand at the small of my back when I was almost to my locker.

"I see you decided to take my advice, Scarlett," Chase whispered in my ear.

I stopped at my locker and turned to talk to him, but he was already gone.

Did he really want to keep this a secret or would he warm up to the idea of an 'us'? To be honest, I wouldn't mind an 'us.'

All of my classes before lunch were easy, so I just paid no attention to the teachers.

I walked out of the room and to the back of the library, after the bell rang.

Chase wasn't there yet so I set down my book bag and waited for him.

I saw him walking towards me so I smiled.

"See, I told you, you would end up falling for me," Chase said with a smile and a wink.

"I think you have a spell on me Chase Wilson," I said.

That was all we said before he was kissing me. Today was just like yesterday; one of his hands was at the small of my back and the other was in my hair. I put my hands on his face today; I wanted to play things up a bit.

After about five minutes, Chase stopped to take a breath of air.

"You look really good in shorts, by the way. You don't look fake with a tan and stuff," Chase said.

"Thanks, my mom said pale always suit me."

"That it does."

I hesitated for a minute. What should I say to him? I learned so much new information this morning

"Elaine wants to have lunch with me, so is it okay if we cut this short today?"

"Uh, yeah, sure. But that means tomorrow will be extra long." He winked.

I decided to call him out on his lie.

"By the way, I know Elaine was your brother's girlfriend, not your best friend's so why did you lie about it?"

He waited for a moment trying to form an answer, I guessed.

"Um, I don't know. I just don't really like admitting Adam is my brother. He is so dark and brooding. And why did you say 'was his girlfriend'?"

He didn't know about his brother's break up?

"Elaine told me that Adam broke up with her yesterday. I don't really know, but Elaine was at my locker telling me about it today. Does she not have friends or something?"

"Uh, not really. She must like you if she confides in you. Anyways, really? They broke up? Great, now I'll have to deal with more darkness at home. Elaine was the only light Adam had."

I didn't want to say anything else, so I grabbed his face and kissed him. I could feel him laugh under my lips.

I was really starting to warm up to him.

* * *

After my 'meeting' I went and sat at an empty table with Elaine. She must really have no friends and I felt bad for her because she had been here for three years with no one to talk too. Well, no one except Adam.

"So how long did you and Adam date?" I asked while taking a bite of my cheese pizza.

"Uh, I think like two years. I don't know. I just really don't want to talk about it."

"Oh, sorry. I'll shut up." I smiled at her.

* * *

After lunch I was really thinking about ditching so I didn't have to see Adam in history.

But I decided against. I needed answers and I was going to get them out of him.

So I at in my two classes that were before history; one was free period, so I had time to think because apparently I couldn't think about things enough.

When it was time for history, I walked into Mr. Tilden's class and smiled at him. I liked him, even though he was on the odd side.

I looked back to where my seat was and sure enough there was Adam.

He was wearing khaki shorts and a white v-neck. Normally, guys never dressed like that.

Chase seemed into the whole cargo shorts with a Rugby shirt thing. I thought it was cute, but Adam's choice of style was way more than cute; it was charming and alluring.

I sat down and looked Adam right in the eye. He just stared at me like he was bored.

I opened my mouth to say something, but the bell rang.

"Alright, class, today I will assign each group with a topic and then you will brainstorm together on how you want to approach it. You will do a presentation and you can use Power-Point, a poster board, or any other idea as long as you run it by me first."

I looked at Adam again. How were we going to do this? I didn't want to be rude, so I guess I'll just go with what he wants to do, though he is a senior in junior history. Maybe I should be the one who brainstorms.

"Alright, now Ms. Claire and Ms. Janet, you'll be doing World War II," Mr. Tilden explained. He went through the rows and then landed on us, just like yesterday.

He looked at his paper. "Ah yes, Ms. Scarlett and Mr. Adam, you will be doing the 'Romantic Era' which are the years 1850-1920," Mr. Tilden made his way back up to the front of the class, "you now have time to brainstorm ideas. Please keep your voices low."

Adam and I looked at each other. I knew I wouldn't be getting any answers today, but on second thought...

"So, I don't really know anything about the 'Romantic Era,' do you?" I asked Adam. I was afraid he would just ignore me or say something really mean.

"Actually, I don't," he replied with his deep voice.

"I think that basically means we are getting an 'F' on this project," I said with a laugh.

He smiled. "Yeah, I guess so. But if you really want to try, I wouldn't oppose." He sounded a lot like his brother.

"Uh, sure. Should we do a PowerPoint, poster board, or do you have an idea that could give the illusion we know what we're talking about?"

"I think we're screwed either way so why don't we just do a PowerPoint to get it over with?" he said coldly.

How did he turn so sour all of a sudden?

"Oh, okay. Do you want me to go tell Mr. Tilden?" I asked the sour boy.

"Yeah, that's fine. I'll be sitting here, not moving."

Was that supposed to be a joke? I smiled at him and noticed him blush again.

I got up and made my way towards Mr. Tilden's desk.

So did Adam like me? But why did he turn so cold all of a sudden? I don't think I said anything wrong.

I replayed my words in my head, searching for something that would trigger a mood swing.

Mr. Tilden was sitting behind his desk playing on his computer; solitaire, nice.

"Mr. Tilden?"

He looked up at me and smiled. "Yes, Ms. Scarlett?"

"Adam and I decided to just do a PowerPoint."

He looked sad. "Oh, you didn't want to do something more unique or creative?"

I hesitated. "Actually, Adam said he wanted to do a Power-Point."

"I'm sure he did." Mr. Tilden looked behind me to Adam who was staring at us.

What did that mean? Was Adam a big slacker? I'll just ask Chase tomorrow during our 'meeting.'

"Uh, actually, could you help explain to me what the 'Romantic Era' is?" I asked. I needed all the help I could get.

Mr. Tilden looked happy. "Well, sure Ms. Scarlett. The 'Romantic Era' is a period of great change. The 'Classical Era' had strict laws, so when the 'Romantic Era' came, everyone was allowed artistic freedom. Composers began to experiment. It was all mostly based around music. Does that help?"

I kind of understood what he was saying, but I was still distracted.

"Yeah, that helps a lot. Thanks Mr. Tilden," I said politely.

"You're welcome Ms. Finely."

I made my way back to my seat.

"So Mr. Tilden said it was okay that we're doing a Power-Point and then I asked him what the 'Romantic Era' was. He told me is basically based around music and composers experimenting with their music." I looked at Adam's reaction, which was still bored looking.

"Alright." That was all he said.

"So how should we do this?" Those were my exact words to Chase about our deal.

"I don't really know. Should we just work on it at school?" he asked.

"Sure, that's fine. Where do you want to meet to work on it?"

"The library is good. They have a bunch of computers, so we won't have to worry about that." It was the most I've heard him say.

"Alright, sounds good. Now the issue is when. I have free period sixth hour."

"I don't so, why not at lunch?" Did he know about Chase and our deal?

"I am busy at lunch everyday." This was torturing me.

"Oh yeah, with what?" He seemed oddly interested.

"That's not really any of your business." He was going too far.

"Well, that's the only time unless you want to stay after school?" he asked.

My mom would never let me do that because no one would be home to cook.

"No, lunch is fine. I'll just be a little late everyday. If that's okay with you?" I said rudely.

"I don't care."

I didn't like this kid one bit. I'll make sure to let Chase know tomorrow.

The bell rang at that moment. Had we been in class that long?

"Alright, so tomorrow at the library, I'll meet you at the front," I said.

"That's fine. But are you sure you don't want me to meet you in the back." He laughed and walked away.

Yeah, Chase was definitely going to hear about this.

* * *

When I got home my mom's car wasn't there. She had made no indication that she would be gone today. She must be at her "man's house."

Instead, a car that I didn't recognize took her car's place.

I opened my car door and made my way towards the house.

I opened the house door and heard the TV on.

"Scarlett! How is my baby sister?" Oliver yelled.

I was shocked. He got up and I ran into his arms.

We hugged for what seemed forever.

"Oliver! What are you doing here? Is the Peace Corp in town or something?" I asked.

"I haven't been in the Peace Corp for over a year. I figured mom had told you."

"Where were you then?" I asked.

"Dad's. He looks great. Runs marathons and everything. You should go visit him this Christmas break or something."

"I might just do that Oliver." I smiled.

We were talking each other's ears off when we heard mom's keys in the door.

I looked at Oliver. "Oliver, mom and I are in a big fight and also, I never told her you apologized." I had to get in that last part so there was no confusion. Oliver looked at me like he hadn't understood what I just said.

Mom walked into the house without her usual greeting. Even when we fighting she would at least give me an acknowledgement. Then I heard her voice. "Scarlett? Whose car is that in the driveway?"

I looked at Oliver, but he winked at me. At least he wasn't mad at me.

"Mom, there is someone here to see us," I ignored her question. She would have to see for herself.

"Well, who is-" she didn't finish her question because she came in eye's view of Oliver.

"Oh, well hello Oliver. How have you been?" she asked.

"Hey mom. I've been good. Just decided to fly down here. The car is a rental," he explained.

"Oh, well that's nice." Why was she being so cold to him? How could you be cold to Oliver? He was so easy to talk to and he was always nice to you even if he was mad at you.

"Yeah, so how have you been?" Oliver asked.

"I've been great," she hesitated, "Scarlett; can I talk with you for a minute, alone?"

"Sure, I guess." Just because Oliver was here doesn't mean I have to be nice to her.

I got up from the couch and looked at Oliver. He shrugged, but then focused his eyes on the TV.

I walked into the kitchen where she was waiting for me. "So what do you need? Sorry, I haven't started dinner. I just got to talking to Oliver and lost track of time."

"Oh, that's fine. I picked up a pizza for us actually," she eyed the box on the table.

She actually got me pizza? Was she trying to show me that she cares?

"Oh, thanks. Pizza sounds great, actually."

"But before we eat, I need to talk to you, if that's okay?" she asked me.

"Sure, shoot." I was eyeing the pizza. Since I've been skipping lunch for my "meetings" with Chase, I was starting to get hungrier.

"Alright, well yesterday, I should have stayed out here and talked, not went into my room. I'm sorry for that. And I just want to say I'm really sorry. I never realized how much I put on you. I am the mom and I should be doing the cooking, shopping, and paying the bills. That sort of stuff."

She was apologizing? I must have really gotten to her. Well, it was about time.

"Uh, its okay mom. I'm just glad you know how I feel."

"But there is another thing I need to say," she hesitated, "I am the mom which means you can't talk to me like you did yesterday. That was totally uncalled for. I mean I consider myself a cool mom because I didn't yell at you for what happened in Huntington," I winced and so did she, "and I give you an easy environment to live in. What I'm trying to say, you can tell me how you feel, but just be polite about it." She ended with a smile.

"I'm really sorry mom. You're right; I should have been nicer about it." I hugged her and I could feel her tense body relax.

"Alright," she whispered, "what is Oliver here for? Did he say why he is here?"

"Yeah, about that. Mom, when you got into that big fight a couple of months ago, I called Oliver and explained to him that you were helping me out and he said to tell you he was really sorry and that he overreacted. I just never told you because we were getting so close that I didn't want Oliver taking you away from me."

She stepped back and looked at me. "You are my daughter, aren't you?" She laughed and hugged me. "Sweetie, I love you and no one, not even your brother will ever take me away from you."

"So you aren't mad at me?" I asked with caution.

"Of course not. But I wished I had known about the apology. I need to go talk to Oliver. Help yourself to the pizza and I bought some soda and put it in the fridge."

"Alright, thanks mom."

She started making her way out of the kitchen.

"Mom, I love you, by the way. I really and truly do."

She paused with her back to me. She turned around and there were tears in her eyes. "Scarlett, my baby, I love you too. I really and truly do." She smiled and turned around to walk away.

I eyed the pizza and then dug in. It was so good, even though it was the really greasy kind of pizza. There was no way mom was going to eat this unless she did a day of cardio afterwards.

Now that my family life is looking good, I needed to deal with the Adam and Chase thing. And I needed to deal with it very soon.

5

Adam stared at me the whole hour. I just wanted it to be over so I could go see Chase next hour. At lunch, I was definitely telling him how his brother was rude. But why would Chase care? After all, he is just using me.

When I entered Mrs. Eisner's class, I saw Chase. He was smiling at me just like yesterday. I really could get used to this place; I just needed to settle things.

I smiled and winked at him; clearly I'm a bad flirt. But he blushed, just like Adam, so I knew I must be better at it than I had anticipated.

This was going to be my tool to get Chase to think about dating me. And I wanted some information. Like what was his secret?

I sat down and realized this was going to be another boring hour of my life that will be wasted.

As I walked to my locker after English, Chase came up to me and kissed me on my neck.

"How is Scarlett today?" Chase asked.

So was he going to talk to me in public? I guess we're making progress.

"I'm great. My brother is in town. And how is Chase Wilson this morning?"

"Really? Your brother? You already want me to meet the family?" he laughed at his own joke.

"Well I would maybe introduce you someday, but you tell me."

"What do you mean?"

How could I put this? "Well, are you open to maybe making this official?" I gestured my hand between us.

He looked confused. "You mean, you really want to be my girlfriend?"

I didn't want to sound pathetic. "Do you want me to be your girlfriend?"

He hesitated and then kissed my neck again. "I would love for you to be my girlfriend," he whispered in my ear.

"Really?"

He stepped back to look at my face. "Yeah, I put that on the table the first day. Like I said, I had just met you, but I knew I liked you."

"So you don't want me to be your girlfriend just so you can get action?" I really didn't have any other way to put it.

"I want to get to know you Scarlett Finely. Everything about you. Can you handle that?" he laughed.

"I think I can manage." I laughed too.

"Alright, well I'll see you at lunch today, gf," he said with a wink.

"Oh, I forgot to tell you, I have to meet with Adam today at lunch, so our "meeting" will be cut short again." What did he think about my meeting with Adam? I couldn't really tell by his expression.

"Why do you need to talk to Adam?" he asked.

"We have this project due for history and he is my partner. We're doing the project on the 'Romantic Era'."

"Oh okay, well be careful around him Scarlett. Once he has you on his hook, you'll never leave you alone."

He sounded just like Elaine telling me about Mrs. Moore on my first day.

"What do you mean?" I asked.

"He is just weird that's all. I'll explain it to you sometime."

"Yeah, he was being really rude to me yesterday. Like he was okay one minute and then the next he went cold." I told him. I looked at Chase's reaction, surprised. He looked mad.

"He was mean to you?" Chase asked.

"Yeah, but don't worry about it. I gave him a dose of his own medicine." I laughed and kissed his neck.

But Chase pulled away. "Chase? What's wrong?"

He took a minute to answer. "Nothing. Its just...nothing. I'll see you later, okay?" He kissed my forehead and walked away.

This family seemed very dysfunctional. I wonder what Chase would say to Adam. Would he tell Adam I told on him? That would make things even more complicated.

* * *

At lunch, I met Chase in our normal spot. His expression was the total opposite of what it was when he left me today in the hall. I had spent the next two periods after English trying to think about what I would do if Adam and Chase got into a fight over me, but I knew I was being silly because no boys would ever fight over me.

"Hey there beautiful," Chase beamed.

"Hey, are you alright?" I hated to bring it back up, but I wanted to know what happened.

"Yeah, peachy. What time do you have to meet Adam?" he said with disgust.

"Uh, I have to meet him in like five minutes in the front of the library."

Alright, what is going on?

"Alright, then we have five minutes to kill," Chase said as he approached me. He winked, smiled, and then grabbed my face with his hands.

If there was anything that could distract me from my day, it was definitely Chase's kisses.

When we stopped to breathe, I could see something out of the corner of my eye.

I turned my head and Adam was just standing there.

"We were supposed to meet ten minutes ago," Adam said not looking uncomfortable.

"Really Adam? You had to interrupt right now?" Chase asked angrily.

"Chill little brother. Scarlett?" he gestured for me to join him to walk to the library.

"Uh, Adam, I'm a little busy with your brother."

I looked at Chase and he was smiling at me. I winked. I was really getting good at this.

"Yeah, it's your choice I guess, but I'm sure Mr. Tilden wouldn't like to hear that you ditched me make out with my brother."

I stepped away from Chase and walked towards Adam. He probably thought I was joining him, but instead I slapped him across the face.

I could hear Chase laugh.

"Don't you dare threaten me Adam Wilson."

I walked back to Chase and kissed him once on the lips.

"Look, I got to go do this project, but do you want to meet me by my car after school?" I asked him.

"Of course. I'll be there," he looked over the Adam, "and by the way Adam, if you ever threaten my girlfriend again or even be the slightest bit rude," I smiled at the word girlfriend, "then I'll do more than slap you across the face."

Chase and I laughed together. How could I already be falling this hard for a guy I just met?

I walked over to Adam and looked him into the eyes. "Shall we?" I mocked.

He started to walk to the library and I sauntered behind him.

***

"Alright, where should we begin? In the 1800s?" I asked Adam.

After I slapped him, we walked the library and neither of us has said a word until now.

"Uh, sure, that's fine," Adam responded.

"Okay, I'll go ask the librarian where I can find some books. I'll be right back. You can start up the computer while I'm gone."

He didn't respond so I walked up to the librarian.

She was a younger woman, probably in her forties. But she was single, no doubt about it. Her eye brows were bushes and her hair struck in every direction.

She looked up from her book. "Yes?"

"Hi, I'm doing a project on the 'Romantic Era' and I was wondering if you know of any books that are on the topic," I asked in my nicest voice. From my experience, librarians were always mean.

"Well of course," she said sweetly, "they are on shelf 400." She pointed to the farthest shelf.

"Alright, thank you."

I started to walk to the shelf. I looked over to the computers where Adam was just staring at our computer.

I walked over to him. "Is it working?"

He looked startled. "What? Oh yeah, it's working fine. I'm just bored."

"Well I didn't ask you if you were bored," I said with a humorless smile.

"Ha, good one," Adam replied.

I could really get used to this whole hating him thing.

I continued on my quest to find some books about the 'Romantic Era.'

Once I got the shelf, the bell rang. How did time go by so fast here?

I went to retrieve my bag to head off to my next class.

Next to my bag, was a note.

Scarlett,

I will be five minutes late after school, so just be patient. Meet me by Adam's red jeep. If he gives you trouble, just let me know.

Chase

When was he in here? I didn't see the note there when I walked by two minutes ago.

* * *

In history, I ignored Adam the whole time Mr. Tilden was talking. But, I could still feel his eyes on me.

When the final bell rang, I roamed around the parking lot looking for Adam, Chase, or a red Jeep.

My eyes landed on Adam's red Jeep, with Adam in it.

I walked over to the car slowly and with caution. Should I say hi? Or act like I don't see him there?

When I got the Jeep I decided to get it; I figured I would make Adam feel uncomfortable, just for my own pleasure.

He didn't look at me surprised, so he must have seen the note before I did.

"Hello Scarlett." He said slowly.

What was up with this guy?

"Adam," I nodded my head, "do you know when Chase will be here?"

"Your guess is as good as mine."

"Oh, okay."

I had been waiting for fifteen minutes when Chase showed up. The whole parking lot was empty except for a few cars. Chase looked bewildered when he saw me.

He kissed my cheek. "Why are you in the car? You could have just stood at the back."

"Uh, I didn't want to take the chance of getting hit by any crazy drivers."

Chase chuckled, "Well I'm glad you thought of that. Shall we?" His eyes flashed to the library.

I looked at Adam who was staring straight ahead and then my eyes went back to Chase. I smiled. "We shall, boyfriend."

When he helped me out of the jeep I decided to leave my stuff there to further piss Adam off.

Chase and I walked towards to library – holding hands.

He turned to look at me. "You know, I really like the sound of you calling me boyfriend. It has a nice ring to it."

"My thoughts exactly." We both laughed.

Once we got to our usual spot, Chase got me into his grip.

After about ten minutes, we heard foot steps.

"God, what now Adam?" Chase growled.

"Uh, Scarlett, your phone rang, and I didn't know what to do so I answered it. It was your mom. She said your brother Oliver is in the hospital and that you need to get down there right now."

Oliver? In the hospital? Why was he there?

"Uh, okay. Thanks. Did you bring my stuff?"

"Yeah, here." He handed me my book bag, keys, and cell phone.

"Thanks," I said while grabbing my stuff.

I looked at Chase. "Uh I got to go. I'll see you tomorrow?"

"Do you want me to go with you?"

He didn't wait for my answer. He took everything and grabbed my hand. We walked to my car where he threw my stuff in the back and helped me into the passenger's side.

If I wasn't crazy with worry right now, I would have probably been charmed by his politeness.

We drove to the hospital as fast as we could.

Chase dropped me off at the front, so he could go and park.

I looked all around the hospital. Where was my mom? Where was Oliver?

"SCARLETT!" I heard my mom yell. I turned around and saw her standing there with make up streamed down her face.

I ran to her. "Mom? What's wrong with Oliver? Is he going to be okay?"

"He was in a car accident. He is in surgery right now."

I hugged my mom as hard as I could.

"He'll be okay mommy, don't worry," I whispered into her ear.

At that moment I heard foot steps.

I turned to see Chase.

I hadn't realized I'd been crying until I felt a wind chill on my face.

Chase took me into his arms and put one hand on the back of my head.

I knew I had some explaining to do to my mom later, but now I needed to be comforted, not to comfort.

For hours I just sat on Chase's lap while he kept whispering that it would okay.

Finally, a nurse came out.

I jumped off of Chase's lap and he grabbed my hand and we walked to meet my mom who was talking to the nurse.

Before I made it to her though, she fell on the ground and starting weeping.

I stopped where I was. I looked at the nurse. She shook her head at me.

Should I cry? Should I comfort my mom? Should I push myself back into Chase's arms? I didn't know what to do. So I did what I knew best; I ran away.

6

I ran for I didn't know how long. It seemed like forever or an eternity, but I knew had been only a few minutes.

How could Oliver die? He was just at our house this morning. He wore his super man pajamas out to the kitchen. I remembered I laughed and called him my baby brother.

"Baby brother? I'm just a fan of the man," he had said with a laugh.

The doctors and nurses must have the wrong patient; there was no way Oliver was dead. I winced at the last word.

And when was I going to start crying? Wasn't that your initial reaction to this? To cry your eyes out and eat a bunch of rocky road ice cream while watching hundreds of sad movies?

But I couldn't bring myself to cry. The only thing I could think about was catching my breath. So I stopped. I was at a dock now.

Doven had a dock? Well this is the first time I've seen it.

At least no one followed me. I didn't want to talk. I just wanted to look out at the murky water.

I also wanted to crawl up into a ball on the ground. I wanted to cry. I wanted to see Oliver again; not his cold, lifeless body. I wanted to know that my mom and I could make it through this; together.

I wanted answers.

Who did this to my brother? Who had the nerve to kill my brother? Did the doctors try hard enough to save my big brother? Who was going to have to arrange his – gulp- funeral? Would my dad come here to comfort us? Or would he merely just send a card?

I finally gave into my wants.

I got onto the dirty dock's ground and I put my knees to my chin and cried. This was what I needed; to cry. I needed to cry for a day. I needed to cry for a week, a month.

I cried so much that I ended up falling asleep on the dock.

I awoke to footsteps.

"Scarlett? Are you okay?" Adam asked.

Adam? Where was Chase? Where was my mom?

And was I okay? I don't think I will ever be okay again.

"Can you take me home?" I blubbered into my knees.

"Of course." He picked me up and carried me back to his car. His chest was warm and he smelled like lilacs.

We drove in silence until he pulled into my driveway.

He turned off the car and he was unbuckling his seat belt. What was he doing?

"Adam?"

"Yes Scarlett?"

"Where's Chase?" I forgot to ask him when he picked me up at the dock.

"Your mom needed," he sucked in some air and cleared his throat, "well, she needed someone. She wouldn't get off the ground so they had to give her some sedatives. Chase stayed there to take her home when she woke up."

"Oh. That was nice of him." I had nothing else to say.

"Scarlett, I know I don't know what you're going through, but I'm here for you. And so is Chase, of course."

He was actually here for me? I'm sure he just felt sorry for me. I don't know what happened, but something ticked and I went into hysterics. Adam got out of the car and carried me to into the house, into my room.

He laid me down onto the bed fully clothed.

What should I do next? Thank him? Hug him?

"Adam?" I didn't know what to say after I got his name out of my trembling mouth.

"Yes Scarlett?" he said with his deep, calming voice.

"Will you stay with me tonight? I don't want to be here alone."

Was that technically cheating on Chase? I didn't want him to stay the night so we could make out. I wanted him to stay with me because I needed to be comforted by his warm body.

I looked up at him. The moon was shining perfectly on his face, his lips...

He looked confused; like he didn't know what to say next. His eyebrows were pushed together almost as if he was concentrating on something.

"You don't have to if you don't want too..." I continued. What was I going to do if he rejected me? Just thank him and let him go? What if he told Chase I had asked him to stay?

"No, I'll stay," he finally responded.

"Are you sure? Because you really don't have to if-"

He put his index finger on my lips.

"Shh, Scarlett. You should get some rest."

So did he want to stay? I don't know why I was so worried about what he wanted or didn't want to do.

He put himself into a sitting position on my bed, so his head was resting against the wall. I put my head on his lap and started to cry again. He stroked my head with his finger tips. Was I going over the line? Or would Chase understand?

I fell asleep again.

* * *

I woke up to an empty bed still fully dressed. Well, at least he didn't take advantage of me.

I got up and grabbed some clothes.

I went into my bathroom and started my shower; I needed to clean myself up.

The hot water felt good against my skin, almost blistering.

Was Adam still here? Or had he left? What about my mom and Chase? If they weren't here when I got downstairs then I would go to the hospital. But how? Chase still had my car.

I turned the shower off, but sat down in the tub. Did I want to go down there? Where everything reminded me of Oliver? Would I burst into hysterics again in front of Adam?

I decided to get up and face my fears. I dressed quickly and brushed my hair and teeth.

I walked down to the kitchen.

Adam was standing over the oven, cooking.

He must have heard me approach him because he turned around and smiled.

"I figured you might be hungry, so I made scrambled eggs and bacon. Is that okay?"

I smiled at him. "Sounds great, thanks. You didn't happen to make a fresh pot of coffee, did you?"

He laughed. "Actually, it's ready right now." He handed me a mug full of steaming coffee. Mmmm, this is what I needed. I took a big gulp of it. It burned my throat, but it tasted too good to spit back up.

"Wow, you're a good coffee maker."

"Years of experience." He winked.

He handed me a plate of scrambled eggs and crackling bacon.

I scarfed it down. Normally I wouldn't have felt like eating like this in front of a guy, but I hadn't eaten since breakfast yesterday morning.

When I was done, I looked up and saw Adam staring at me, smiling.

"You must have been very hungry. Would you like some more?" He pushed the skillet towards me.

"No, I just ate enough to feed a small army. But thanks, I mean, for everything."

He looked at me for a few minutes without saying anything. What was with the staring?

"Uh, you're welcome, for everything." He smiled.

I blushed. I wasn't supposed to be falling for him. I liked his brother not him. I needed to keep telling myself that.

"So what's the news? Is my mom coming home today?" I asked.

"Chase said that he would probably bring her here at around 5 because the sedatives need to wear off before she is allowed to come home."

"Oh, alright. So, what now?" I asked. So what now? Should I tell him to stay until they come or should I let him go home?

"Um, if you want me to stay, I can. I just smell really bad." He laughed.

He definitely didn't smell bad. He smelled like a field of flowers.

I could let him take a shower here, but what would he wear? I could let him change into Oliver's clothes.

"Well, you are welcome to take shower here. I can get some of Oliver's clothes for you." I winced when I said the name aloud.

He noticed. "Are you sure? Because I can run home and take a quick-"

I put my hand down on this hand. "Please, just stay."

What was I doing? I should be forcing him out of here.

He looked down at our overlapping hands.

"Alright, just point me to the bathroom."

"Its right there," I pointed with my other hand to the first door on the left down the hallway, "and let me go get you some clothes."

I raced up the stairs to the laundry room. I opened the dryer where I had thrown a load in before school yesterday. I pulled out one of Oliver's flannel shirts – you needed them to live in Washington- out of the dryer with a pair of his sweats. Oliver and Adam looked to be about the same size so I don't think that will be a problem. Should I get him boxers? That would be the right thing, right? I pulled out a pair of Oliver's boxers, hoping for a pair that didn't have anything resembling cartoons on them. I got a pair with stripes of them. That should be appropriate.

I ran down the stairs and knocked on the bathroom's door.

"Hold on," Adam yelled through the door.

When he opened the door, he had no shirt on.

I couldn't help but stare.

Dazed, I handed him the pile of clothes.

"Uhh, he..re," I stuttered.

"Um, thanks," he said while grabbing the clothes, "I'll try not to be long."

"Oh, don't worry about that. Take as much time as you need."

He closed the door and I walked back to the kitchen to sit down before I fell. Did he mean to have his shirt off? But why would he do that? I wanted to call Chase, but I had no idea what his phone number was. I looked around for something that could distract me and I landed on a phone. A phone? I didn't recognize it. I got up and walked over to the counter where it lay.

I picked it up and opened it. It was Adam's. I went through the contacts until I landed onto Chase's name. Should I call? What if he answered?

I pushed send. The ring came on and I waited impatiently. I needed to get through and talk to Chase before Adam caught me using his phone.

I froze. Did Chase know Adam was here? I doubt it. What would be my lie to get out of this one?

"Hello? Adam? Is she okay?" Chase asked on the other end. I relaxed. So he knew Adam was with me.

"Uh hey, Chase, it's me. Scarlett. I'm just using Adam's phone."

"Scarlett! Are you okay? Of course you aren't okay. That was a stupid question, sorry."

"It's okay. No, I'm fine. I was just calling to hear your voice," I lied. I didn't even know why I called, to be honest.

"Well, I'm glad you did. I love hearing your voice too, girl-friend."

I felt a pinch of guilt when he said that.

"So is she okay? My mom?" I tried to change the subject.

"Yeah, she's fine. She is sleeping right now. But I'll come over later to drop her off and we can talk then. Does that sound okay?"

"Yeah, I can't wait to see you Chase." More lies.

"Alright, I'll see you later. Goodbye Scarlett."

"'Bye Chase."

I hung up the phone and heard a noise.

I turned to see Adam staring at me, with wet hair.

"Oh hey. Sorry, I used your phone. I just needed to check on my mom."

"That's fine," he moved to stand next to me so I handed him his phone back, "how is she?"

"Chase said she is still sleeping. So not much of an update."

He nodded.

"So..." he said.

"You want to watch a movie or something?" I asked. I needed to get out of this awkward situation.

"Yeah, that sounds great." He smiled.

* * *

During the whole movie I watched Adam's face. He was watching the TV screen with such intensity. Finally, I heard music for the credits. He turned to look at me.

"That was a good movie," he said.

"Was it? I wasn't really paying attention."

He laughed. "Yeah, so do you want to watch another one or what?"

"Uh, I need to get the mail and pick up my mom's dry cleaning. Do you mind?"

"No, I don't mind. Would you like me to drive?"

"Sure, that would be great."

We both got up to put our shoes on.

He grabbed his keys and we headed out the door.

When we got in the car he turned on the radio.

"What do you like to listen too? Are you a metal head or purely classical?" He laughed but I couldn't laugh. I don't think I would ever be able to laugh again.

He stopped once he saw my reaction.

"Uh, I can just turn the radio off."

"Yeah, the silence would be nice."

He put his hand to the radio and pushed the 'off' button.

I was clearly making him feel uncomfortable when all he was doing was trying to be nice to me.

He pulled out onto the street and started to drive slowly.

"Adam…" I turned to look at him.

He looked at me but didn't say anything.

"I just wanted to thank you again. For last night. For this morning. For everything. You are so nice to me and I'm just so rude to you. I just have this thing where I try to keep people out of my life. I let my guard down with Chase, but I let it down too early. What I'm trying to say is I'm sorry. You're a great guy and you shouldn't be associated with me, with my past, with my dysfunctions, and with my flaws."

He pulled onto the side of the road.

"Scarlett. Why did you just tell me all of that?"

Why did I tell him all of that? But was I ready to tell him how I liked him more than his brother, more than any guy I've ever known?

"I don't know." I tried to fight back the tears.

He took my chin in his hand. I looked into his eyes.

But then, suddenly, he dropped it and drove back onto the road. What did that mean? Was that supposed to be a rejection? But I don't think I really even offered anything.

We drove to the post office first, then to the dry cleaners. Adam didn't say one word and nor did I.

When we got back to the house, I tried to get out of his car as fast as I could. I couldn't tell if he was following me or if he had even gotten out of the car at all.

I went into my room and sat on my bed, facing the window.

After about five minutes, I heard foot steps behind me.

I didn't even want to turn to see who it was so I just kept staring out the window at the neighbor's house, the sky, the yard, the sun.

"Scarlett..." Adam said slowly and quietly.

He sat on my bed and put his arm around my waist to pull me closer to him. I started to cry. Every time he held me, I went into hysterics.

He didn't try to kiss me. He just laid my head onto his chest. Oliver's shirt held both Adam's scent and Oliver's. After I came to that realization, I cried even harder, if that was possible.

Would I ever get through this? Would mom make us move again to a place with no trace of Oliver whatsoever?

Unlike Chase, Adam didn't say anything to me to comfort me. Just his body heat was comforting enough.

I fell asleep against Adam's warm, hard chest.

Chase shook me awake. My head was lying on a pillow so Adam must have moved before Chase got here, smart move.

"Scarlett? It's me, Chase. I'm here. Your mom is here too."

I shot my eyes open. My mom? Where was she?

"Where is she?" My voice was hoarse.

"She is in her room sleeping. The doctor gave her some pain killers. She probably won't wake up until tomorrow."

"What time is it?"

"It's about 5 PM. Adam said you feel asleep after I talked to you. You slept for a long time."

Wow, I must have been asleep for what six hours? There was no way I would be able to sleep tonight.

"Is Adam still here?" I asked. I knew I shouldn't have asked that.

"He left, when I came. We are doing it in shifts. Its my turn." He smiled.

"Oh okay."

He sat down and pulled me into his lap. Apparently I was lighter than what I had thought.

The only thing I knew to do with Chase was kiss. So I kissed him. At first he was confused, but then realized, I didn't really want to kiss, I just wanted to know someone was here for me.

He laid me on my back and held himself over my body. He took his shirt off slowly, but I left my clothes on; I wasn't ready for that yet. I had his face in my hands while he moved one hand to my back. He switched it so he was lying down and I was hovering over him. He kissed my lips, then my jaw, then my collarbone and finally made his way to the middle of my stomach.

I tried to pay attention to only his bare chest; kissing every inch of it.

I fell asleep after I got to one hundred kisses.

7

I smelled sizzling bacon when I woke up with the next morning. How in the world did I go to sleep? I felt like all I was doing was sleeping.

I went into the bathroom and brushed my hair slowly; I wasn't in a hurry to see whoever was down there this morning.

I brushed my teeth counting each stroke.

What about my mom? Was she awake? I needed to see her, so I headed out of the bathroom and into my mom's bright pink room; she would always paint the day we moved in.

She was lying on the bed fast asleep. I could even hear a faint snore. Those must be some powerful pain killers. If she got to numb the pain, shouldn't I be allowed to also?

I walked over to her dresser to find the right prescription bottle out of the many bottles that sat here; my mom had a lot of problems.

I found the right one. I looked at the instructions and it said two pills daily. Well I didn't want to sleep, so one would be okay. I opened to bottle and popped one in my mouth. I noticed some of the side affects on the side of the bottle.

They included drowsiness, nausea, hair loss, heart attack...why did I just take this terrible pill? I should have read the side affects before I swallowed it.

Well, it was done, so maybe I should go face Chase or Adam.

As I made my way down the stairs I realized, who did I want to be down here? Chase? But I had fallen asleep on him last night which means I should be embarrassed, but I wasn't.

Adam? But I haven't spoken a word to him since yesterday after my little speech.

Why was life so difficult? Couldn't the bacon be cooking itself and I wouldn't have to deal with either of them?

When I got to the end of the stairs I was somehow not surprised; Adam was standing over the oven just like yesterday.

"So Chase takes the night shifts when I'm sleeping, but you got stuck with the shift where you actually have to talk to me?" I smiled at him after he had turn to see me.

He smiled with warm eyes. "Well good morning to you too, Scarlett."

"Good morning Adam. But seriously, you don't have to cook for me."

He frowned. Did he like to cook for me?

"But, if you wanted too, I wouldn't oppose," I confirmed with a smile.

His frown turned back into a wide grin. Good, I actually fixed something.

"Coffee is right here," he said after I had eyed the pot.

He handed me a steaming cup. Just like yesterday, I chugged this one down.

He passed me a plate full of bacon and scrambled eggs.

"Wow, thanks," I said with a smile.

"You are certainly welcome Ms. Finely."

Since when did he call me Ms. Finely? Is that why he smiled the first day in history when Mr. Tilden called me that?

I froze. School. What was I going to do about school? Mom was in no shape to call and tell them the bad news and what if they didn't believe me, a student?

"Adam, what should I do about school?" I blurted out. Why was I asking him?

He pulled his eye brows together again.

"Um. I could call in for you and act like your dad?" he asked with a smile.

"Wow, that's very...illegal." I laughed. Here I was laughing when yesterday I never thought I could laugh again.

He looked surprised that I was laughing too, but he smiled and forced out a chuckle.

"But, no seriously. What should I do?" I continued.

"I'll handle it. Don't worry about it."

"You just met me and you're handling things for me? Wow, you are a nice guy." I smiled.

He seemed like he was concentrating on something. "So, what should we do today? I'm here until 5. Then you have Chase."

"Are you sure your parents are going to get mad at you guys for spending the whole day and night with me? Which brings me to my second thought, what about you going to school? What is it, Friday? You should be in school."

He looked like he was forming an answer. "Yeah, it's Friday. But I figured if you needed someone here, I would let Chase

74

go to school. He is the one with promise." He laughed at his joke.

He was here because he thought I needed someone? Well, he was right, but I didn't want him to get into trouble.

I didn't say anything so he asked his question again. "What should we do today, Scarlett?"

The painkiller was starting to work because I was definitely feeling drowsy.

"Uh. Let's watch some more movies. I'm kind of tired," I said.

Should I tell him about me taking a painkiller?

"Alright. Would you like me to pick one out?" he asked.

"Yeah, sure. Its all yours." What was I saying?

He looked at me for a minute, but then walked over to the movie shelf.

I tried to get up, but failed miserably. I was sprawled across the floor doing nothing. Not laughing, not crying, and not smiling.

Should I tell him about the painkiller just in case? In case of what, I wasn't sure.

He came back and found me on the floor. He ran over to me and carried me like a groom caring a bride on the first night.

"Scarlett, are you okay?" he asked once he had me on the couch.

"Yeah, I just took one of my mom's painkillers. Its no biggie."

Well I guess so much for not telling him. But I couldn't stop myself.

I felt nothing. My whole body was numb. I didn't have anymore thoughts. My mouth felt like it could talk for hours, though.

"What, you took one you of your mom's painkillers?" he asked angrily.

"Yeah, but like I said it's not a biggie." I had no idea what I just said.

He got on his knees so he was eye level with me.

"Scarlett, it's a huge deal. Are you feeling okay? Are you drowsy? Nauseated?" he asked worried.

"I'm fine. I can't feel anything. I'm just a little drowsy." The pitch of my voice went high at the end.

"You need to sleep it off then. Do you want to stay here? Or should I take you to your bed?"

"No, here is fine."

"Alright. I'll be right over here, in the chair, if you need me. Okay Scarlett?"

"Yeah. But can you promise me two things?" Should I really ask him what I'm about to ask him?

"Uh, sure, I guess."

"One," I held up my index finger, "don't tell Chase about this. It will be our little secret. And two," I put up two of my fingers, "don't ever leave me Adam Wilson."

His eyebrows went up at the end like he was surprised. Was he surprised? He shouldn't be. I basically professed my love to him yesterday in the car.

"Uh Scarlett. You don't know what you're saying, so I'll just sit over here."

He got up and sat on the chair across from the couch.

"But I do know Adam! I know everything I'm saying, damn it!" I yelled.

"Alright, Scarlett," he said slowly like I was going to drop a bomb at any second.

I didn't speak through the whole movie. I just stared blankly at the screen. I wanted to take a peek at Adam's face, but I couldn't move my body. Apparently, these painkillers are supposed to make you feel paralyzed.

When it was over, Adam came and sat on his knees so we were eye level again.

"Are you okay Scarlett?"

"I can't move my body Adam. Is that normal?" I asked worried.

"Yeah, sort of," he said with a chuckle.

"Please don't laugh at me."

He stopped immediately. "Sorry. So what do you want to do now?"

"Take me to my bed, please." What was I going to do when I got there?

He stood and picked me up.

"I'm not too heavy, am I?" I asked. I didn't want him to have to lug a cow around.

He laughed, but then stopped remembering my request. "Scarlett, you are literally as light as a feather."

"Well, that's good at least." I smiled at him.

When we got to my room he gently set me on my bed.

So where should I start? "Adam, sit, please." I guess there.

He obediently sat down waiting for what was coming next.

"You asked me what I want to do next."

"Yeah…" he hesitated.

"Well, I'm ready to tell you about my past, if you're willing to listen."

* * *

He sat there the whole time and listened to where I've moved and how my mom slept with her boss. Then I told him about how Oliver got caught smoking in the bathroom; we both laughed at that part. I told him about how my dad never called me. I then told him about how I never was friends with anyone and how I needed to take a risk. I told him about Casey and Demetri. I told him about how his brother was blackmailing me, but how I ended up liking him.

And then I ended with one last line; "Adam, I don't deserve a guy like you."

I kissed his cheek and fell soundlessly asleep.

* * *

When I woke up the sun was still shining so I knew Adam was still here.

Had the painkiller wore off yet? I tried to get up and succeeded, though I was still a little groggy.

I tried to remember everything that had happened before I fell asleep.

I told him about everything and had I kissed him? I couldn't remember.

I went into the bathroom and took a shower.

When I got dressed and cleaned up, I walked down the stairs.

Adam was lying on the couch, sleeping. So I'll guess I'll make something to eat. I looked at the clock – 2 PM – well that's good. I had three more hours until Chase showed up.

I went into the kitchen and found a frozen pizza in the freezer. I started the oven and got a pan out.

When I finally got the pizza into the oven, I heard foot steps.

"Scarlett..." Adam said. I didn't turn around.

He walked over to me and put his arms around my waist. Alright, we were definitely going over the line. But I felt so safe in Adam's arms.

I knew if I turned around, then I was telling him that I liked him. But I couldn't figure out how I could fall for him so fast. Maybe, I just had mixed feelings; he was taking care of me. Yeah, I'm sure that's it. But he was here, not Chase.

I turned around and looked into his eyes. They looked pained like he wasn't sure this was the right thing to do.

I put my hands in his hair, but I didn't move my face any closer; I wasn't sure if I was ready yet.

Was I ready yet? Did I want to cheat on Chase?

I kissed his neck; it was too late for Chase.

He kissed the exposed skin on my collarbone.

"Scarlett, do you want to go up to your room? Or do you want me to stop?" he asked into the hollow at the base of my throat.

"My room."

He picked me up like he had before and we made our way up to my bedroom.

Wait, what about my mom? She was in the next room. She could wake up at any moment.

He laid me gently on my bed and took his shirt off. I copied him.

I had done this a million times with Demetri, but this felt more powerful with Adam. I definitely didn't feel like this with his brother last night.

He hovered over me and kissed every inch of my body; my face, my neck, my chest.

I flipped it us so I was hovering over him. He stared at me, awed. I kissed every muscle on his flat stomach. I kissed every muscle on his rigid arms. I moved over to his neck, his collarbone, and I landed on the hollow at the base of his throat.

He stopped me and looked into my eyes. "Are you sure you want to do this Scarlett?"

I couldn't speak. Shouldn't I say yes? This is what I wanted, right? But I couldn't say anything.

I looked down at this chest and then back into his eyes.

"Adam, you should go."

He laid me gently on my back and got up.

I turned so I was looking out the window.

I could hear him doing something. What was he doing? At that moment I felt a blanket on top of me.

"Scarlett, you are wrong. I don't deserve someone like you," he said and then walked out.

After a few minutes I could hear his car pull out of the driveway.

I broke down.

I could feel every single tear fall down my face. Each tear representing the pain, guilt, and regret in my life.

Pain for the death of my precious big brother.

Guilt for what I had just done to two amazing guys.

And regret for coming to this small, wretched town.

"Scarlett, I'm here." I recognized Chase's voice at once. Was he going to ask where Adam went? Did he already know about this afternoon? If he knew, he wouldn't be here.

I turned over to face him. My face felt weird because all of my streaming tears had dried on it. The shirt I had clumsily put on after Adam left was damp with the tears that made it passed my chin.

"Hey, Chase."

"Are you alright? Adam said you were a little depressed today."

"Yeah. I'm fine. Is my mom awake?"

"She went to the funeral home. They called and said they needed her to make the arrangements as soon as possible.

"Oh, okay."

He hesitated in the door way unsure if he should come in.

"Scarlett," he walked over and sat on my bed, "I'm here for you. You know that right?"

Why was he asking me this?

"Of course Chase. And I'm glad you're here; I don't think I would be able to get through this without you and...your brother." I hesitated on the last couple of words.

"I'm glad to here that." He smiled at me.

"Chase, you can go. I won't be much of a conversationalist because I'm sort of tired." I was tired; but tired of sleeping, tired of seeing people, and tired of saying I was fine.

He looked at me intently, but nothing like how Adam stared at me.

"No, I want to stay here with you. I don't mind the silence, honestly."

I ignored him and turned to look at the dark sky. "So, you aren't mad at me for last night?"

"Of course not. It's not about that for me; you know that. And plus tomorrow is Saturday, so I talked to Adam and I got the day shift so we could hang out." I could hear the smile in his voice.

"Oh, so Adam isn't coming tomorrow?" I asked. I wanted Adam back, but I didn't know what I would say to him.

"Uh. He said he would be here on Monday." I could hear the pain in his voice. I turned to look at him.

"Oh okay." I knew he knew now.

"But it's okay if I get you all weekend, right?"

I got up and went downstairs. I opened up the front door.

Chase came down the stairs and looked at me and then the door. "Oh."

He put on his shoes and went through the doorway, but turned around.

"Scarlett, is this it? Are we over?" Chase asked with pain in his eyes.

I walked up to him and grabbed his face with my hands. "Chase, you're way too good for me."

I kissed his lips and then his forehead. I couldn't feel any tears in my eyes. Shouldn't I be crying?

"Scarlett, don't do this."

"This is the last time you will see me. My mom and I are going to move; it's inevitable. Go find another girl; one who actually deserves you."

I turned and walked back into the house; without one last glimpse of him.

* * *

When I got inside I checked the clock – 6PM – so my mom should be on her way home.

At that moment, I heard her keys in the door.

She was wearing a black jogging suit with her blonde hair up in a pony tail.

"Hey mom," I said when she saw me.

"Hey honey. How are you doing?" she asked. She seemed fine; she must have some pain killers in her right now.

"Honestly?" I paused. "I actually feel okay."

My mom looked around worried. "Where is your friend, Chase?"

I did not want to explain this to my mom right now. "We broke up."

"Oh, that's too bad. I liked him," she said with a frown.

"Yeah, me too. So are you hungry? I can make you something," I said.

"No, I'm not really hungry." She started to head up the stairs, but turned around. "Honey, I forgot to tell you, the visitation will be tomorrow night. And the funeral is on Sunday." I could see that she wanted to end it at that.

"Alright, thanks mom."

She started to race up the stairs again.

Was I going to have to move us myself? Or could I call my dad for some help? What about mom's 'man'? Where was he?

I heard a knock on the door. Who could that be? If it was Adam what the hell was I going to say?

I ran to the door and opened it.

"Hey honey. How are you doing?" my dad asked.

"Dad!" I ran into his arms like I had the night Oliver arrived here.

He smelled like the outdoors – his usual scent. "I'm doing fine, by the way. Better than mom."

"Yeah, that's usually how it is. Where is she?" he asked while looking around.

"Come in, come in," I grabbed him and took him into the kitchen, "she is upstairs, crying I think. She had to go down to the funeral home today and make the arrangements. The visitation is tomorrow night and the funeral is on Sunday," I said really fast. I didn't want to talk about this when my dad was in my house. I hadn't seen him since mom sent Oliver and I up there for Christmas when we lived in Illinois.

He looked at my face like he was expecting me to burst into tears at any moment. "Oh okay. Look sweetie, I don't mean to put you on the spot, but I just got here and I didn't even think to get a room at a hotel. Is it okay if I crash on your couch?"

He didn't think to get a hotel room? He must be really upset if he was willing to sleep under the same roof as my mom.

"Of course Dad. You can stay as long as you want. Though, I don't think we will be here for much long."

He looked at me with a questioning face. "What? Are you moving already?"

I wanted to change the subject. "We'll talk about it later. I'll go get you some blankets."

I raced down the hall to the linen closet and pick out two quilts.

I came back into the kitchen where my dad stood where I had left him.

"Here," I handed him one, "you can help me make your bed."

We walked together to the living room. Once we got his 'bed' set up, we walked back to the kitchen.

"Are you hungry dad?" I asked him, ready to pull out a frozen pizza from the freezer.

After the thing that happened with Adam today, I didn't even think about the other pizza I was in the process of making. I headed to the oven and opened it. It was gone.

What happened to it?

"Actually, I've starving," he said while patting his flat stomach.

"Yikes dad, you need to eat. It looks like you are going to be all bones soon."

He chuckled. "No, I'm just watching what I eat."

"Would a frozen pizza be okay? I don't want you to gain weight while you're here." I winked at him.

"I think I can manage. And a pizza sounds great." He smiled.

I got the pizza out and tore the wrapper.

"So… how long are you here for?" I asked while setting the pizza in the oven and turning it on.

"I don't really know kid. I just want to make sure you guys are okay before I leave."

"We're doing fine dad. You don't need to worry. I have some good friends checking on me everyday." Did I have some good friends checking on me everyday? I don't think Chase will come back, but maybe Adam will come.

My dad eyed me. "Really? You've already made some friends? That's good."

"Yeah, I know it's shocking." I laughed. Well, I'm glad I can laugh again.

"No, it's not that. It's just that when Oliver came up and visited me, he told me that you weren't doing too well. He said you had some trouble at your last school. But you seem okay to me."

"I am okay. Yeah, I kind of lost who I was in Huntington, but I recovered and now I'm fine." I turned to look at the living room.

"Oh, well, that's good. I'm glad kid."

"Dad. There is something I need to talk to you about."

"Shoot Scarley." I never liked his nickname for me, but he thought it was cute.

"Uh well, I need someone to talk to the school. You know like to tell them?"

He looked surprised. He must have thought I was going to talk about something else. "Oh, well sure I can call. Do you want me to ask for them to let you stay out of school for a while. How long were you thinkin'?"

"I hadn't really thought about that. I don't want to be out too long, though."

"Don't worry about that. Take as much time as you need."

"Alright, thanks dad. But seriously, you don't have to stay any longer than the funeral. I mean I love having you here, but you need to get back to work."

He laughed. "Don't worry about that either, Scarley."

"So, do you want to watch a movie or something? Mom won't be up for a while because the doctor gave her some pain killers."

He looked very surprised now. "Pain killers? They shouldn't give her those."

"Well, I don't know much about it. So anyways, what movie?"

He looked sidetracked. "You go pick one out. I need to go talk to your mom. I'll be right down though."

I didn't think it was the best idea for him to go talk to my mom. That would just make her more upset. "Dad, maybe you should wait until tomorrow."

"Scarlett, go pick out a movie. I will be right down," he said sternly.

I watched him walk up the stairs and to my mom's room.

What did he need to talk to her about? Did I just get her into trouble because I told dad about the pain killers?

I checked on the pizza and then went to the movie shelf. Without looking, I just grabbed one. I was trying to listen for my dad's voice because it was such a low octave, I could probably hear it going through the floor. But I didn't hear anything.

I put the movie in and waited for it to load. The movie didn't look familiar, but I pushed play anyways. The beginning credits began.

What time was it now? It felt like only five minutes had passed.

I went into the kitchen and looked at the clock – 7:30 PM. How did time go by so fast here?

Just then I could hear my mom's bedroom door shut.

My dad came down the stairs looking like he regretted going in there – I didn't blame him. My mom was scary when she wanted to be.

"So, how's mom?" I asked cautiously.

"She is doing fine. Not as good as you, but still fine. What movie did you pick?"

"I don't know. I just picked one and put it in," I admitted sheepishly.

He smiled, but didn't laugh his normal booming laugh. "Alright. I'm heading in there. Would you like to join me?"

"Actually, I'm going to wait until the pizza is done. But go on ahead."

"Alright. Just don't be long kid. I don't want to be some pathetic old man who gets stood up by his own daughter." He smiled.

"You're not old and I am not going to stand you up." I smiled back at him.

He turned around and made his way to the couch.

I opened the oven door, but the pizza still wasn't done.

I wanted to go check on my mom, but I didn't want my dad to know that I was checking on her.

"Dad, I got to go get something out of my room, I'll be right there!" I yelled the lie.

I ran up the stairs not waiting for an answer.

I went to my mom's door and opened it without thinking about knocking first.

She was sitting up, but facing the wall so I couldn't see her face.

"Mom? It's Scarlett. Are you okay?" I asked. Of course I knew the real answer, but I was waiting for her to respond like I had to everyone who asked me that.

"Honey, I don't think I will ever be okay ever again"

I walked over to her and sat down.

"Same here," I admitted.

She turned to look at me. She didn't look like she had been crying.

"Well, you're hiding it well." She patted my hand.

"Yeah, sure I guess."

"Tell me something to take my mind off of this whole thing," she said while staring at her hands.

I leaned back to look at her. I had thousands of things to say to my mom. I wanted to tell her that I think I'm in love with a guy I just met, but I've already hurt him. I wanted to tell her that I secretly resented my dad for never calling. I wanted to tell her I had cheated on my boyfriend with is brother. Sure, I had a lot of things to tell my mom.

"Mom, I know you probably want to move, but I can't. We can't. We need to stop running. We need to make it through one place with out running from something." I had never known I felt like this until the words were out.

I wanted to move, but I couldn't. I needed to settle things here. I didn't want to make my mark and leave. I wanted to have a life here.

She looked up at me. "Honey, I think that's the smartest idea you have ever had."

I pulled her into my grasp. I wanted to hug my mom forever.

After about five minutes, I realized I needed to get downstairs. I pulled away from her. "I have to go be a good hostess to dad. And I'm making a pizza so you're welcome to come and get some at anytime." I kissed her forehead and got up.

She didn't say anything so I closed her door and headed downstairs.

I looked into the living room and my dad was asleep on the couch.

Wow, either the movie I picked was really bad, or he was just really tired.

I went into the kitchen and straight to the oven.

The pizza looked perfect – nice golden crust with the cheese all melted.

I pulled it out and started to cut it.

I don't think I've ever been this hungry in my entire life. I dug into a piece with both hands.

I heard a knock on the door.

If it was either Adam or Chase, I was closing the door. I wasn't ready to talk to them.

I went to the door and opened it slowly.

"Scarlett!" Elaine squealed.

"Hey Elaine," I said quite not as excited.

"Scarlett, I heard the news. I'm so sorry. Is there anything I can do for you?"

"Uh, no. I'm fine thanks. But if you're hungry you can join me for some pizza?"

"Pizza sounds great, thanks."

She came in and we walked to where I had left the mauled pizza.

She eyed it and started to laugh. "You must have been really hungry."

I laughed with her. It felt good to hang out with someone that I didn't have an emotional connection with.

"So how has Algebra II been?"

"It's been the same boring subject. I think Mr. Rainer has gotten even creepier."

So she noticed he was creepy too?

"Oh yeah, I noticed that on the first day." I smiled at her.

She laughed and we continued with our conversation until she realized that her parents were going to ground her if she didn't get home soon.

I told her I would be at school soon, so she needed to save me a spot at her lunch table.

After she drove out of my driveway and onto the street, my dad woke up.

"Hey Scarley. Who was that? One of your good friends?"

"Yeah, actually. She is a really good friend."

He smiled and grabbed a piece of pizza. There was only one piece left. I picked it up and put it in the microwave so if my mom wanted it, it would be ready to warm up.

My dad and I watched another movie together, but he fell asleep so I headed upstairs to get some sleep too.

As I lay in bed, my mind wandered. What if Chase showed up tomorrow? What if Adam did? I don't think I was prepared for either of them.

I fell asleep thinking about what lay in store for me tomorrow.

9

I woke up to the sound of a lawn mower. I ran to my window to see my dad mowing the lawn.

I got dressed in some jean shorts and a deep red v-neck shirt.

I ran down the stairs and out to the yard.

I tapped his shoulder.

He stopped the mower, startled.

"Scarlett? Is everything okay?" he asked with anxious eyes.

"Yeah, everything is fine, but why are you mowing my lawn?"

"I didn't realize this was your lawn. I thought it was the-" he stopped after I started to walk back inside.

He hadn't changed one bit. He had always acted like a child, even when I was one myself. He would be the dad who would come out of the toy store with more stuff than the kids.

I went to the kitchen. This was the first day since three days ago that I hadn't woken up to the smell of bacon and eggs.

The clock said it was 11 AM. I must have been really tired even though I sleep later than that in the summer.

Shouldn't my mom be up by now? At that thought, I ran up to her room.

When I entered though, she wasn't there. Where was she now?

I heard the shower start. Aha, my questions have been answered.

Mom said the visitation was tonight, so I had a while to prepare.

I needed to prepare to see my brother lying in his casket, lifeless. I needed to prepare to see all of the weeping people. I needed to prepare for all of the hugs and 'I'm sorry for your losses.' I needed to prepare to see Chase, if he would come. I needed to prepare to see Adam, if he would come also.

What would I say to either of them? Before I fell asleep last night, I had not figured anything out.

My stomach growled at that last thought. Alright, I need to eat something.

I went to my fridge and found a sandwich already made. Who was it for? I didn't want to take the chance of it being for someone else and then eating it. Right next to it, though, was an apple. I guess an apple would tie me over for a while.

I grabbed the red fruit and washed it off. Before I could take my first bite, my dad came into the house.

"Hey kid! That's my apple!" he yelled.

"I'm sorry. I didn't realize this was your apple," I said with a smug smile.

"Alright, you got me. But seriously, I was planning on eating it."

"Well, I'm hungry. So do you have anything in mind on what I should eat?" I asked.

"There is someone out there for you. That's what I came in here for. So you can't eat until you talk to him," he said with a wide grin.

Someone was here to see me? But I looked terrible. "Who is it?" I asked.

"I don't know, kid. I didn't ask for names. He asked if Scarlett was awake and I said yeah and then I told him to wait here while I go get you."

I ran upstairs to brush my hair. It wasn't doing anything for me, so I put it up in a ponytail. This should do for whoever the guy was.

I ran back down stairs, but stopped at my front door. I needed to put on my best face.

I opened the door and saw him standing there.

"Hey Scarlett. I didn't wake you, did I?" Chase asked.

I exhaled. "No, you didn't wake me. Our mower, however, did." I eyed the mower that I didn't even know still worked.

Chase looked at it and laughed. I joined him.

"So, did you need something?" I tried to ask in my nicest voice.

"Uh, I just wanted to make sure you were okay, ya know, with the visitation and everything today."

"Oh. I'm good. I don't think its really hit yet, though."

"Yeah. So who was that guy?" he asked while pointing to the house.

I looked back at my house where I saw the kitchen curtain flutter. My dad was seriously spying on my? He was definitely going to pay for it when I got back in there.

"Oh," I said while turning to look back at Chase, "that's my dad. He is in town for the visitation and funeral."

"Ah, I see."

"Yeah. So I was wondering, if you wanted to maybe go with me to the visitation? I mean my mom will have my dad and I'll have…" I didn't have anything to say to end the sentence.

Chase was staring at the house, but now he looked at me, stunned.

"Yeah, of course I'll go with you. Do you want me to pick you up or meet you there?" he asked. I hope he didn't think I wanted to get back together with him.

"Uh, can you pick me up?" I really didn't want to ride in the same car with my mom and dad. I didn't know if they would fight, but there would definitely be tension.

"Sure. What time?"

"Um, well the visitation is at 6, but we have to be there at like 5:30, so is 5 okay?" I hope I wasn't going to be super early.

Chase smiled. "Alright, I'll be here at 5."

I had to smile back at him. "Alright, thanks Chase. I see you then."

I turned around and walked back into the house.

I could hear his car pull out as I walked back into the kitchen.

My dad was standing at the counter by the sink with his back to the window.

"Hey dad, I'm catching a ride with Chase to the visitation."

"Oh okay. Are you sure you don't want us to take you?"

"No thanks. I don't really want to be in the car with you guys." I laughed at my joke and my dad joined in.

I eyed the apple on the counter where I had left it.

He saw me. "Go ahead. You already got your germs on it anyway." He winked at me.

I grabbed and started to make my way up the stairs, but turned around.

"Hey dad, next time you want to spy on me, make sure you're not obvious about it." I smiled at him.

"Alright kid. I'll take that into consideration."

I ran back up the stairs and into my room.

* * *

I could wear a black shirt with a black skirt, but what if the blacks didn't match.

I was having no luck in finding an outfit. Normally I would throw anything on, but I wanted to look nice for this.

Are you supposed to wear all black to the visitation?

What about a black sweater with a white skirt that had black detailing on it? Alright, that would have to do.

I grabbed the clothes and threw them on my bed.

Now what about shoes? Heels were definitely out. My mom said I had to wear them tomorrow, so I wasn't going to suffer tonight too.

I looked at the bottom of my closet and saw a pair of black slip-ons. Those would have to do, too.

After Chase left, I had went up to my room and devoured my apple. Then, I fiddled around and cleaned my room. Now it was 3 PM and Chase was going to be here in about 2 hours; I needed to hurry.

I went into the bathroom with a robe; I'll just get dressed in my room tonight, I thought.

I started the shower and waited for it to heat up.

When I got in, it felt amazing. The hot water was steaming all around me. The water numbed my body; I needed to be as numb as possible with out taking pain killers.

I covered my hair with my fruit flavored shampoo; it was Oliver and my favorite. I needed to think about only Oliver today. This was about him, not me.

After I was done with my shower, I brushed my hair and blow dried it.

I continued with the hygienic process by brushing my teeth.

I went into my room where my outfit had been ironed. Mom or dad?

I got dressed and put my shoes on.

Should I put some make up on? I figured a little eye liner and mascara wouldn't hurt.

I went back into my bathroom and put on as little make up as I could.

If I cried, it wouldn't smear or run that badly.

What time was it now? I went downstairs and checked the clock – 4:45 PM.

This town seriously had a problem; time went by too fast.

I went into the living room and turned the TV on. Where were my mom and dad? I guess they already headed out for the visitation.

Just then, I heard a faint knock on the door; Chase was early.

I opened the door to Chase wearing khaki pants, a light blue button down shirt, and a dark blue tie.

"I'm so sorry I'm early," he said politely.

"Oh, its okay. I was ready anyway." I smiled at him.

I grabbed my purse that held my phone and my house key.

"Let's go," I said while heading out the door.

We got into his car and headed to the funeral home.

Neither of us spoke the whole way there.

When we got there, though, there was a line. I recognized a lot of the people that Oliver had gone to school with. It was surprising how many people would come all the way down here.

Chase and I walked by all the people and into the building.

My eyes landed on the casket. Without thinking, I grabbed Chase's hand. I looked at him with pained eyes.

"Its okay, I'm here." He pecked me on the cheek. Yeah, he definitely thought we were getting back together.

I guided us up to where my parents were standing. My dad's expression was impatient and my mom's was worried.

I let go of Chase's hand and went to hug both of them.

"Broke up my butt," my mom whispered when I hugged her.

At that moment, the funeral home director came up and asked us if we were ready to open the doors. They were starting really early.

When my mom nodded with a yes, the guy went and asked everyone to form a line and make their way up to the front, where we were standing. I was definitely not ready for this. I grabbed Chase's hand again, but didn't look at his face this time.

The first woman was a friend of my family's when we lived in Washington.

The next was one of Oliver's old classmates.

After that, a lot of the people were from the Peace Corp.

One person that I noticed wasn't there was Adam. Why didn't he come? Did he think I didn't want to see him?

When it was all over, I released Chase's hand and I went to the bathroom.

I looked at myself in the mirror. I hadn't shed one tear during the whole visitation.

My mom was crying and my dad even welled up a few times, but I didn't even have the urge to cry. Was it because I had cried so much the first couple of days?

I went back out to where we were all standing, but everyone was gone. Where had they gone too?

I went over to Oliver's casket and just looked at him. My parent's put him in an outfit that almost looked exactly like Chase's. Oliver really needed a hair cut. His hair was on his face. I couldn't let him look like that so I reached my hand out and brushed the hair back. I almost expected him to open his eyes and laugh, but he didn't.

I could feel the tears now. There was no point in fighting them back. These were the tears that burned your throat. I gasped for air. I was sobbing. Finally, I got my request; I cried like everyone else did.

"Scarlett? Why don't I take you home?" Chase grabbed me by the waist and pulled me up. I hadn't even realized I fell to the ground.

Chase didn't look as strong Adam did, but he carried me out to the car like Adam had done so many times.

He set me in the passenger side door and ran around the front to get into his side.

The whole time we were driving back to my house, Chase was holding my hand.

Did I want Chase to hold my hand? He was being nice so why couldn't I accept his kindness? I left my hand where it was, but I made no notion of holding his hand back.

* * *

When we got back to my house Chase carried me up to my room. By this time, the crying had stopped, but I couldn't speak.

After he got me settled in, Chase laid on the bed with me. He had one arm over my waist and held me to his body while I was turned to look at the dark sky.

"Scarlett," he whispered in my ear, "do you want me to come and get you tomorrow for the funeral?"

I nodded my head. What was I doing? Shouldn't I go with my parents?

"Alright, well I have to go. My parents were expecting me awhile ago. Your mom said the funeral started at 2 tomorrow, so I'll probably be here at 1:30. Is that okay?"

I nodded again.

"Alright. Good bye Scarlett. Try to get some sleep tonight." He kissed me behind my ear.

After a couple of minutes, I heard his car drive away.

I broke down today, so would I break down tomorrow too? Oliver looked so alive I don't think I could handle seeing him again. What about Adam not showing up? Did he really think I didn't want to see him or did he figure that he barely knew me, so why come? That was probably it.

Either way, I had to prepare again for tomorrow.

10

"Scarlett, its time to wake up," my mom whispered into my ear.

I sat up too fast. "Good morning to you too, mom." I smiled at her.

"Sorry, sweetie. I just wanted to make sure you had enough time to get ready. I laid your outfit out," she did a head tilt towards my chair that sat in the corner.

There was a pair of black heels and a simple sleeveless black dress. It was scoop neck, so I didn't have to worry about anything showing.

"Oh, thanks mom."

"Your welcome. I also thought that maybe I could curl your hair. You know, like big spirally curls?"

"I see we are making up words again." I smiled at her. "But no seriously mom, you don't have too."

She frowned. "Well I thought you would want to look nice for Oliver."

I put on my best fake smile. "Mom, I would love for you to dress me up today."

She smiled with warm eyes. "Great! Alright, well you need to take a shower and then I'll blow dry your hair and everything. I'll even do your make up."

I got up and grabbed my robe.

She followed closely behind. "Now, you need to hurry. Your hair is long, so it will take longer to blow dry and curl. Snap, snap!" She pushed me into the bathroom and shut the door.

I started the shower. I needed to be numb again.

I got in and sure enough, I was numb within seconds. I knew my mom was only dressing me up because she needed to keep her mind preoccupied, but she was going a little far.

I got out of the shower after I could feel my body tingle a little. The heat was definitely going to blister my skin if I didn't get out soon.

As soon as I turned the shower off my mom knocked on the door. "You have two minutes to brush your hair, brush your teeth and get dried off!" she yelled through the door.

I did as she said in under a minute; I was a little afraid of her right now.

She came in with all of her tools i.e. curling iron, hair spray, blow dryer, and her bag of make up.

"Sit on the toilet. I guess it will have to do."

I sat there silently while she blow dried and curled my hair. Then I didn't dare to make a peep when she was putting my make up on.

When she was done, she looked satisfied. "Now you need to go get dressed. I put my pearl necklace on your dresser. Put it on. You will kind of look like Audrey Hepburn." She winked at me.

I did as she said. I put on my camisole and then the black dress. At least it had a side zipper on it so I could zip it; I would be too afraid to ask her to zip it because she would probably yell the whole time or not by gentle.

I slipped into the heels and then put on the necklace. I walked over to the mirror.

Wow, my mom really knew how to make average look amazing. When she was doing my hair, I was afraid it was going to be all frizzy and poufy, but it looked sleek and shiny. And then when she was doing my make up I could have sworn she put clown paint on, but all she put on was a little mascara and eye liner. It looked way better than when I had done it yesterday.

I walked over to her and hugged her. "Thanks mom, it looks great. Now, its your turn to get dressed." Her make up and hair were already done.

"Your welcome sweetie and don't be so pushy." She laughed at her own joke.

I knew it was all a ploy, but I laughed along with her.

I left her alone to get dressed and I went downstairs. The clock said 1:15, so Chase should be here at any moment.

Just then, my dad came out of the guest bathroom.

"Yikes dad, you could actually pass for a gentleman." I smiled at him.

"Ha ha. Could you help me with the tie, though?" he asked.

I didn't have much experience with tying ties, but I got his tied within seconds.

"There, looks great," I said while patting his shoulder.

"How about you Ms. Hepburn?" he asked with a chuckle.

"All mom's doing."

"Ah." He nodded.

"Elizabeth! Lets go!" my dad yelled up the stairs. "Are you ready kid?" he asked me.

"Actually, Chase is coming to get me. That's okay, right?" I knew I didn't need to ask him, but I felt I should anyways.

"Sure. I guess we'll meet you there." He kissed me on the forehead. "Tell your mom I'll be in the car."

He headed to the door and outside.

My mom padded down the stairs at that moment. She was wearing a black blouse with a black skirt. It would probably have looked terrible on someone else, but my mom pulled it off.

"He is in the car." I pointed outside.

"Alright. Are you coming?" she asked while holding the front door opened.

"Chase is coming to get me," I confirmed again.

She looked surprised. "Oh, alright. I'll see you there honey."

"Alright mom. See ya."

She closed the door behind her. I could here the car door shut and then the car pulling out of the driveway and onto the street.

Chase was going to be here at any second, so I just stood in the kitchen and waited.

I heard a knock at the door. Normally I would have ran to get it, but the heels made that impossible.

I swung the door opened.

"Hey, Scarlett. You look great, even though that is totally irrelevant," Chase babbled on.

I was beginning to notice that he did this when he was nervous.

"Hey Chase and uh, thanks." I smiled at him.

"Shall we?" he gestured toward his car.

I grabbed his hand for support. Support from these heels and support for what I was about to endeavor. "We shall."

We walked silently to the car.

"Alright, would you like some music?" Chase asked while pulling out of my driveway.

I looked at the radio. I never liked music in general but I needed something to distract me. "Uh sure, but it's your choice." I smiled at him.

"You'll regret that," he said with a wink.

At that moment rap music filled the air. I wasn't surprised, but Chase never gave off the impression that he liked rap music.

During the whole ride to the funeral home, I stared at Chase. I never noticed, but he had a little peach fuzz above his lip. He also had impeccably clean ears.

When we got there, the music stopped.

I started to get out, but Chase's arm sent a shock through me.

I shuddered, but he didn't seem to notice.

"If you wait one second, then I can help you out." Chase smiled at me. Wow, his dimples were really something.

He got out and sprinted to my side of the car.

"Alright, careful." He gestured his hand out.

I grabbed it and tried very gracefully to get out – it didn't work. Chase caught me before I could fall.

"Sorry, these heels aren't the best for someone so uncoordinated like me." I looked up and smiled at him.

"Its okay," he said with a chuckle.

He grabbed my hand and we made our way towards the entrance of the funeral home.

I saw my mom and dad at the front, crying.

I squeezed Chase's hand and made my way up to them.

"Scarley, its time to say goodbye before they close it," my dad said through tears.

"Alright, can I have a minute by myself though?" I needed to be alone for this.

My parents looked at each other and then nodded.

"Sure sweetie, that's fine," my mom said.

They walked together to the back of the funeral home where the director was.

I glanced at Chase. "I'll be back there," I gestured to the back, "in a couple of minutes." I kissed him on the cheek and he made his way to my parents.

I turned to look at my brother's lifeless body. I waited for him to just open his eyes.

"Ollie, wake up. Please just wake up," I said to him.

I put my hand on his chest, but couldn't feel a heartbeat.

This was it. I knew it was over; there was no chance of him ever hugging me again, punching my arm, or even just smiling at me from the across the room when one of our boring relatives got a hold of him.

I needed to say goodbye, but I didn't know how to do it.

"Ollie, I love you. I know you can hear me where ever you are. Make some room for me because I'll be joining you some-day." I bent down and kissed his cheek.

I left one tear on his pale cheek.

This tear represented my goodbye.

* * *

"Alright, I think we're ready to start," my dad whispered to the funeral director.

The director nodded and passed the information.

I could hear the sad, depressing music begin.

My family plus Chase made our way to the row of chairs in the front.

"Squeeze as hard as you need to," Chase whispered in my ear.

I turned and smiled at him.

The pudgy pastor walked up to his podium. "Although I didn't know Oliver, he seemed like a kind man. These past couple of days I've been told numerous stories of his happiness, kindness, and his warm heart," he took a deep breath. "Today we are here to say goodbye to Oliver's body, but not his spirit. He has touched every single person here and there he shall stay."

I couldn't listen to this anymore.

Oliver was dead, but the pastor was edging around the word. Just say it! I screamed in my mind.

"...and now, its time to lay the body to rest," the pastor continued. He stepped down from the podium and walked over to Oliver's casket. He put his hands on the top and prepared to shut it.

I didn't see the rest. I jumped up and ran out of the building.

This was it. This was going to be the death of me. I ran to the end of the parking lot not knowing what I should do or where I should go.

I felt a hand on my waist. "Scarlett, I'm here," Adam whispered into my ear.

I leaned my head back so it was resting on his shoulder.

He wrapped both arms around my waist and held me tight.

"Where have you been?" I barely got out of my mouth.

"You needed time to think, to prepare."

He knew me too well. But how? We've known each other for less than a week and he was seeing me at my worst.

I turned around and hugged his waist.

Just then I heard footsteps. Oh no, I already knew who this was.

"Adam? What the hell do you think you're doing?" Chase yelled.

But Adam didn't drop me and I certainly wasn't going to let go of him.

"Chase, she needed someone," Adam said into my hair.

"Yeah, I know. I kind of thought I was her 'someone', but apparently not."

I dropped my hands from Adam's waist. "Its okay," I mouthed to him.

I turned to look at Chase who was just standing there with his eyes narrowed at his brother.

"Chase, I'm really sorry. You were here for me and I appreciate that."

"Is this why you broke up with me?" Chase asked incredulously.

I could see Adam look at me startled. Did he not know I broke up with Chase?

I didn't know what to say. "Uh, yeah. I mean yes. I'm sorry Chase. I didn't mean for it to happen."

Chase didn't say anything; he just walked to his car and drove away.

I looked back to Adam.

He looked surprised and troubled. "I need to go."

"What? Why? You just got here." Why was he leaving me?

"This was a bad idea, I'm sorry Scarlett."

He started to walk away, but I grabbed his hand. "I broke up with him for you and now you're leaving me?" I was dumb founded.

He refused to look at me. "I'm sorry Scarlett," he paused to form an answer, "I'll see you at school when you come back."

He yanked his hand from mine and walked away.

I fell to the ground. This was not a good day for me.

"Scarlett, sweetie? Are you okay?" my dad came running out to me.

"I'm fine," was I'll I could manage before the tears came.

He picked me up by the waist and tried to hold me up.

"Scarley, we have to go to the burial site now."

My mom came out at that moment and helped my dad get me to the car.

Once they strapped me in, I was out.

***

"We're here," my mom whispered in my ear.

I opened up my eyes to my mom's face smeared with mascara. "Alright, give me a second to get ready," I said hoarsely.

"Okay honey, but don't be long." She started to walk with my dad to where everyone was standing by Oliver's grave.

I got up and got the mirror my mom left on her seat.

There was nothing smeared and my hair was nothing to scream about. I thought I was going to look like a monster. My mom really must have put on all bulletproof make up and hairspray.

I threw the mirror on the seat and opened the car door.

I tried to get out as best as I could with these heels on – thanks mom.

I started to walk gradually to my parents.

Was I ready for this? Was I ready to say goodbye to my brother? No, I wasn't, I decided. But I had no choice, I had to do this; I had to say goodbye to my brother; the guy who I knew was there for me. The guy who was always going to be my best friend. And the #1 guy in my life.

Once I got to them, the pastor finally started.

They waited for me? Now I feel bad.

"Alright, so its time to lay Oliver's spirit to rest," the pastor began.

I looked behind me and saw a bunch of the Peace Corp people weeping. I looked over to my parents and they weren't that far from weeping.

"...now you can say your goodbyes," the pastor finished.

My parents gestured for me to go first, but I wanted to be the last one, the one with the most time.

My dad held my mom's hand and guided her to my brother's casket.

I sat down on the folding chair that was provided and I waited and watched every single person look at Oliver's casket, start to cry really loudly, but then walk away.

Finally, it was my turn.

I got up and walked to his casket.

"Oliver, its time to say goodbye, but don't worry, I'll be here visiting you often."

I patted the flowers on his casket and started to make my way back to the car.

I could hear footsteps behind me.

"Alright Scarlett, we're ready to go," my parents said in unison.

Oliver is dead and my life at school is ruined; maybe I needed to rethink not moving.

11

[2 weeks later]

"Mom, I think I'm ready to go back to school," I confessed.

My mom looked up from the book that she was reading – that was her thing now. "Oh, okay honey, but are you sure? You can take as much time as you need."

I looked down at my hands, nervously. "I've actually been ready for about a week. I just wanted to stay here with you and dad."

"Well then, I'll call the school tomorrow and tell them you'll be returning on Tuesday. Does that sound okay?" she asked.

"Yeah, that sounds perfect. Thanks mom." I got up from the couch and kissed her on the cheek.

"You're welcome," she yelled as I made my way up the stairs.

Alright, I've had 2 weeks to prepare to go to school again. At least I won't be behind in school – thanks Elaine.

I knew I had one friend when I got back to school. I hadn't seen Adam or Chase since the funeral. And my dad decided to stay with us for a while. When I asked him about his job he told me that there was more than one doctor in Washington.

After about one week of grieving I knew I was ready to go back to school, but I wasn't sure if I was ready to see the people there.

I told my mom that maybe it wouldn't hurt if I stayed home for another week.

But the whole week I did nothing but clean and watch movies while mom read and dad did outside work.

I was actually surprised at dad because back in Washington he would always just hire people to do the yard work so when he turned the weed whacker on for the first time here, I knew something bad was inevitably going to happen; but nothing did. He was surprisingly a good yard worker.

And now here I was, going back to school on Tuesday. I had butterflies in my stomach much like the ones on my first day about 3 weeks ago.

Would Chase continue to black mail me or would he just forget the deal because he was disgusted by me? Would Adam give me a nod of acknowledgement? And what about the history project? I had looked at my syllabus a couple of days ago just to make sure I wasn't behind and the syllabus said that it was due in two weeks which meant that Adam and I needed to get to work.

I knew I was over thinking all of this, but if you had cheated on your boyfriend with his older brother you would be worried about seeing them both after an absence due to your brother's death, right?

I guess I'll will just have to see what happens on Tuesday.

* * *

"Alright, you can do this," I kept saying to my reflection in the bathroom mirror.

Yesterday I spent the whole day picking out the perfect outfit and getting my homework done.

And now here was Tuesday.

I ran down the stairs and found my dad cooking eggs. "Morning sweetie, I thought you might like some breakfast today." He smiled with warm eyes.

"Yeah, I was actually coming down to eat a bowl of cereal, but eggs sound great." I needed to say anything to keep my parents in the good mood they had been in since the day after the burial.

After we had all drove away from the cemetery, my mom and dad didn't say a word. My mom was too busy bawling her eyes out, my dad was trying to comfort her while driving and I, well I just stared out the window wondering when this madness would be over with.

My dad set the plate of scrambled eggs in front of me. "Do you want some bacon too?" he asked.

I looked up at him with a smile, "no, dad, this is perfect."

I scarfed down my eggs because I had to be at school early to set up things with the principal again.

I ran back up the stairs and brushed my teeth.

"Have a nice day, honey," my mom said from her room. She must have heard my loud foot steps.

"Love you mom," I yelled while running back down the stairs.

"Later dad," I said while making my way out the door.

I got into the car and drove away, out of sight of this little house with our 'little' secrets.

It was nice to see what was beyond my yard. Every time we needed something for the past couple of weeks, dad would just automatically volunteer to go to the store and get it. I would want to go, but he would leave at the crack a dawn; a time I was never up.

Once I got to school, I turned off my car and sat in the silence.

I've been hearing this silence for the past 2 weeks. I needed noise. I needed chaos; in a biblical sense, of course.

I opened up my car door and headed for Mrs. Moore's office.

"You can do this," I whispered to myself.

I opened Mrs. Moore's door and she was unsurprisingly already here.

"Oh, well hello again Ms. Finely. How have you been?" she said after hearing me come in. She was doing the remorse face to me; I guess I'll have to get used to that. Every teacher I had was inevitably going to give me this face.

"I've been fine, Mrs. Moore, thanks," I said with a warm smile. I wasn't going to give anyone of these people something to feed on.

"Well that's good," she paused to look at Mr. Morris's office, "he is running a little bit late, I'm afraid. Can you wait a couple of minutes?"

I glanced at his office and then back at her. "Of course, Mrs. Moore."

After about five minutes of waiting – good thing I got here early – Mr. Morris showed up.

He looked surprised to see me. "Oh, Ms. Finely, I'm sorry I'm late. This time at home is a bit crazy, with kids and all." He was giving me the face already.

"Oh, its okay."

"Alright, Mrs. Moore can you hand me the absentee paper, please?"

Mrs. Moore looked around her desk, flustered. She finally found it. "Oh, here it is." She handed him a bright yellow paper.

"Alright, so bring this back to either Mrs. Moore or me, whoever you find first, at the end of the day. You just need to get every teacher to sign it saying that you've accepted their homework from when you were gone."

"Uh, actually I have it all finished. Elaine Sellers brought it to me at the end of each week."

Mr. Morris looked at me like a student here had never done this before. "Oh okay, but regardless, I just want to make sure. You can have them sign it after you hand your homework in." He seemed like he was proud of himself for thinking of that on the spot.

"Alright, thank you Mr. Morris." I was sucking up big time.

He turned around and went back to his office.

"Mrs. Moore, what time is it?" I looked around to see if there were any students here yet.

"It about 8:00 which means school is starting in ten minutes."

"Alright, thanks Mrs. Moore."

I turned around and walked out the way I came from.

I needed to get to my locker and then to Mr. Rainer's class without seeing either one of them. I was really hoping for Elaine so then they both wouldn't come to talk to me.

At that moment, Elaine answered my prayers.

"Scarlett! I'm so glad you're back. I need someone to talk to at lunch." She hugged me and then matched my pace of walking.

"Hey Elaine, yeah, I'm glad to be back too. Do you want to walk to Algebra II together? I need to stop at my locker first, but then we can go there."

"Yeah, of course. I was just headed that way."

We walked together to my locker while she babbled on about her weekend. Normally I would have looked for a way to get out of this, but recently Elaine was becoming a fairly interesting person to listen to.

"...and then yesterday everything was boring here until Adam had a little blow up in history," Elaine finished.

"What do you mean by a blow up?" I asked.

"Well I heard that Mr. Tilden asked to see what he had gotten done on the history project and Adam said he hadn't done anything because you weren't here to help him. But then Mr. Tilden said that he needed to at least try to do some of the stuff and then Adam just started to like full out yell at him."

"What was he yelling?" Why would Adam blow up at poor Mr. Tilden with his stringy little beard and odd personality?

"Apparently something about how this school was a joke and having to do work for two was ludicrous. I don't really know. But he got like suspended."

"For how long?" I realized maybe I sounded a bit too interested.

"Uh, I think like a week," Elaine said while staring at the cloudless sky.

After that, we walked in silence to my locker and then to Mr. Rainer's class.

I waved to her as she went to sit in her seat and I handed in my homework.

"Mr. Rainer?"

He looked up, bored. "Yes?" after he had seen who it was he turned his whole focus on me, with the face I might add.

"I have the homework for the past 2 and half weeks," I said while handing him the stack of math pages I had done.

"Oh, well thank you. Did you have trouble with any of it?" he asked while setting the papers on his desk.

Of course I had trouble on it. I always had trouble with math. "Uh, no. It was pretty easy, I guess," I lied.

"Oh, well that's good," he said with a smile, but he still had the face on.

At that moment I remembered the absentee paper.

"Uh, Mr. Rainer?" I asked.

"Yes Ms. Finely?"

"Mr. Morris said that you need to sign this so he knows that I've done the homework." I handed him the bright yellow paper.

He quickly signed it and handed it back to me.

"Thanks," I said graciously.

I turned and walked to my seat. At least I didn't have to worry about Adam today or for a couple of days for that matter.

The class went by in a breeze because my mind was else where. Why would Adam yell at Mr. Tilden? And why would he yell at him about our project? Should I just do the project and put Adam's name on it?

But now I had to go see Chase and I certainly wasn't ready for that.

I walked out of Mr. Rainer's class and to my locker to put my Algebra II book in it.

You can do this, I said in my thoughts. I didn't want to say it out loud and have people think I've gone crazy.

"That was so boring. You seemed preoccupied, though. Are you alright?" Elaine asked while walking up to my locker.

"Yeah, it was definitely boring. No, I was listening, but I just wish I hadn't been," I said with a laugh. Elaine joined me.

"Alright, I'll see you at lunch," I said to Elaine before walking away.

"Alright, see ya!" she yelled after me.

I walked quickly to Mrs. Eisner's class. Not because I wanted to be there, but because that woman frightened me.

"Hello Mrs. Eisner." I had trouble pronouncing her name.

"Oh, hello Scarlett. How are you?" she asked with the head tilt. Also a sign of remorse, I have learned.

"I'm fine, thank you." I handed her my homework.

"Oh, I'm glad Elaine got the homework to you," she said with a smile.

I've never seen her smile and I didn't want to again. Either she was a smoker, or just very bad at keeping up with hygienic duties.

I turned away from her and began to walk to my desk.

There he was, but only this time he wasn't smiling at me. And he was definitely not winking at me. Instead, he was looking at his desk scribbling on it.

Alright, that's fine. I guess that's better than a disgusted face.

I sat down and didn't look back once.

When the bell rang, I got out of there as fast as I could.

I went to my locker quickly to escape from him. Even though I couldn't see him, I knew he had been staring at the back of my head the whole class. I could just feel his eyes on me. I didn't know if he was giving me the death stare or what, but I knew they were there.

"Scarlett, we need to talk. Is after lunch okay?" Chase asked me while walking up to my locker.

I kept staring at my locker and at the books; I wouldn't dare took a look at his charming face with his charming dimples.

"Uh, okay. I'll try to cut my lunch with Elaine short, no promises though. That girl has a mouth that could talk for hours on end." I laughed and turned to smile at him.

His expression was anything, but a smile. "Alright, do whatever you need to do."

Before I could say anything else he was out of sight.

* * *

Spanish and Biology II went by in a flash, even though I was watching the clock the whole time.

"Today has been totally boring," Elaine complained once we got food and sat at an abandoned table.

"Yeah, tell me about it." Today has been anything, but boring. First I hear about Adam's suspension and then Chase asks me to meet him at lunch.

Which brought me to my question, what did Chase want to talk to me about? Was he going to want to continue our deal? Or would he just tell everybody about my past? I didn't really care if anybody knew anymore. They all gave me the head tilt and face so I might as well get a few whispers and points.

"Scarlett?" Elaine shook my arm.

Back to the present. "What?"

"I asked what you were doing this weekend. I figured we could hang out or something."

"Oh, sorry, I am busy all weekend. Maybe next weekend or something?" I was lying threw my teeth. But why was I lying?

Elaine looked down at her hands, sad. "Oh okay."

I glanced at the clock on the wall. I had to meet Chase in less than five minutes.

"Uh, Elaine, I'm sorry, but I have to go to the library. I'll see you later." More lies. Soon enough I was going to get used to it and not have to feel this gut wrenching guilt in my stomach. Why didn't I tell her about Chase? I would have definitely lied about Adam, but not Chase.

She looked at me like I was speaking foreign. "Oh okay. I'll see you later I guess."

I got up and threw my untouched food in the garbage.

I started to run to the library, but I didn't know what I was running too.

12

Once I got to the back of library, I was out of breath.

I sat down and put my head between my knees, just like the first day.

You can do this, I thought. You can definitely get through this 'meeting' without freaking out. If he hated you, he wouldn't have asked to talk to you.

Chase's voice interrupted my thoughts. "Scarlett, I'm glad you came."

I smiled at his words, but then looked at his face. I don't think he meant it literally.

"Uh, hey Chase." Just be nice Scarlett, just be nice.

"When I met you, I thought you were just some pathetic new girl who wouldn't know what hit her, but when we started talking and having our 'meetings'" he paused and did air quotes, "I started to realize that I really actually liked you. And then when your brother died I was mad at whoever would do this to you, to cause you this pain. I wanted to be there for you Scarlett. I really did. But when I saw...him...holding you and looking at you like...like that, I couldn't handle it. Don't get me wrong, I'm not here to apologize. I'm just here to tell you that he is no good for you Scarlett and I don't want to hurt you anymore. I don't want to blackmail you."

For the first time I really got to see who Chase was. I saw this terrible pained expression on his face. It reminded me of when I had told Adam to go.

He started to walk away, but I grabbed this beautiful boy's hand.

"Chase, I'm so sorry. I really did like you and I hope you know that. I knew it was quite possible that I could love you." I could feel the tears in my eyes. "I'm sorry."

I didn't dare look at his face. I kept contact on his shoes.

"'Bye Scarlett." He grabbed my hand and kissed my palm, but then he let it go.

I could hear his footsteps until the sound vanished. I couldn't see anything. Not with my eyes filled with these tears. I needed to balance myself on something. I tried to find something near me, but I couldn't. I dropped to the ground and then started to sob.

No, you can't do this Scarlett, I thought.

* * *

I couldn't go to class, so I skipped the rest of school. I knew I would get into trouble, but at this point I couldn't really care less.

And here I was, driving around.

I didn't know where I was going, but I kind of had a place in mind.

Before I had left, I went into the library and found the phone book. I thought it was pretty odd a school library had a phone book, but who am I to judge? I found the address I was looking for and I hopped in my car and drove away.

Now, I was entering a small subdivision.

The houses here were nice and homey like. They weren't like the new subdivisions where all the houses look alike and you didn't know which house was which.

I slowed my speed to look at the numbers on each house.

706, turn head, 707, turn head, 708, turn head, 709; the house I was looking for.

I pulled into the slant-like driveway and turned my car off.

I realized I was hyperventilating.

Calm down Scarlett. You can do this. You can certainly do this.

I took one deep breath and opened my door.

A part of me was telling me to get right back in, but the other part was telling me to get my ass into that house.

I walked up to the bright white door and knocked.

After a few minutes, no one was coming to the door. Should I knock again?

Before I could decide, the door opened.

"Uh, hey, Adam," I managed to get out.

"Scarlett, what are you doing here?" His face looked like he was distracted.

"Um, actually I have no idea." I laughed nervously. This was too awkward.

"Well, do you want to come in?" He turned to so I could walk past him.

I walked by him without saying anything.

He walked by me and pushed the trash off of the couch. "Sorry it's such a mess."

"Oh, its okay." I sat down with a moment's hesitation.

"So Scarlett," he started while sitting in the chair across from me, "do you know yet?"

"Do I know what?" I asked in confusion.

"Um, why you're here?"

I don't think he meant it to be rude, but it came off that way.

"Uh, well, I came back to school today," I was looking around his house nervously. The inside was definitely butch. It looked like a woman hadn't lived here for years. There were dead animals on the walls and the couch was dark brown leather. I turned to see what Adam was watching on the TV before I came. But when I saw the TV, it was turned off.

I looked at Adam, but then blushed because I realized that he was watching me.

"And I heard about your, um, suspension." I finished.

He looked puzzled. "So that's why you came? Because of my suspension? "

I needed to recover from this. "No, I came because I didn't know where to go. I sort of...skipped my classes after lunch?" I said it like a question.

"Scarlett Finely, I am shocked. Why did you skip school?" he asked it like he was already tired of listening to me.

"I had a run in with your brother." I looked down at my hands; they were shaking uncontrollably.

"Ah, the little brother. How is he?"

"Didn't you see him this morning?" I asked.

"No, he is staying with one of his friends. And when my dad asked why he said 'I just study better there and I get more homework done.'" He laughed humorlessly.

"Oh," was all I could get out.

"I think we both know that's not the reason," he said condescendingly.

Why was he acting like this? He was being so cold-hearted, much like how he had acted while discussing our history project.

"What should we do about the history project?" I blurted out.

He was taken back by my bluntness. "I hadn't given it much thought, to be honest."

"Well, do you just want me to do it? I don't mind; I need something to keep me busy," I offered.

"No, you don't need to do it all." I could see his body relax a little.

"Alright, so should we work on it after school? I mean I can come over here when I'm done with school or do you...?" I really didn't know how to finish the sentence.

"Uh, yeah, that's fine," he started to get up, "so I'll see you tomorrow after school?"

I got up and followed him to the front door.

"Yeah, that sounds like the plan." I looked at him and smiled; he finally returned it.

He was holding the door open for me now. "Alright, I'll see you later Scarlett."

I walked out the door and turned around to face him. "Yeah, see ya Adam."

I turned back to my car and walked to it quickly.

One down, one to go.

* * *

"SCARLETT MARIE FINELY GET IN HERE NOW!!!"

I could hear my dad's yell from where I had been sitting in the driveway for the last 5 minutes. So I guess the principal had called my parents.

My dad must have been watching for my car since the call because I could see the curtain flutter.

I hesitantly got out of my car and into the house.

He was sitting at the kitchen table tapping his fingers on it; something he did when he was very, very mad.

When I was younger and visiting my dad for Christmas break, I had learned of his temper.

"Here, just play with this for a while," he had said while handing me some markers and a piece of paper. For about an hour I had just sat at his small wooden kitchen table, drawing. But when he came back to check on me, he had finally realized that the piece of paper he gave to me was a patient's file he was studying. I remember how he threw the markers across the kitchen and screamed a line of profanity.

"Uh, hey dad, how was your day?" I asked with a smile. I decided I was going to act oblivious.

"Skipping school? Really Scarlett?" He was standing now almost face to face with me.

"Uh, I have a good reason?" I lied. Now I needed to make up a good excuse. I could tell him that I was too sad and I needed to leave, but I don't think he would believe that. I could also tell him that I needed to talk to my history partner, but he would have asked who it was and why they weren't in school. I was completely backed into a corner.

"Oh yeah? And what's that?" He still seemed mad. Wow, I guess it was going to take him a while to fully calm down.

I exhaled loudly. "Alright dad, you caught me. I was feeding the homeless." I started to laugh at my own joke, but then stopped once I realized he wasn't laughing with me.

"Truthfully dad, I skipped school because I was depressed - because of Chase - and I needed to get out of there. So I left and went to see, do you remember Chase? Well I went and saw his brother, who just happens to be my history partner. Anyways, I went and saw him to work out our schedule to finish the history project. So you see dad, I skipped school because of a bad reason, but then I made up for it by doing school work."

I knew my story wasn't going to work, even though it was true. My dad was probably thinking of all the mental health doctors that he knew that I could go see.

"Oh, well, you are still grounded. I can't believe you skipped school! If you weren't ready you should have told us." I went and sat back down at the table.

"Yeah, I know. But I actually have to go to his house everyday after school to work on the project," I blurted out. I knew dad was never going to let me go to his house so I would just have to ask mom.

"Whose house?" he asked confused.

"My history partner, Adam. I have to go to his house for like an hour everyday after school for the rest of this week. That's okay, right?"

"I guess, but as soon as you get to his house, you call me. I will be timing you, young lady."

"Alright dad." I started to head up the stairs.

"Check on your mom for me, would you?" he asked.

"Yeah, sure, that's fine."

I ran up the stairs and to my mom's room.

She was reading a different book than last night. Her sweats were dirty and it looked like she hadn't taken a shower for a couple of days.

"Hey mom," she looked up from her book and set it on the bed, "how was your day today?" Hopefully dad didn't tell her about my skipping school.

"Oh, it was good. I finished a book and I'm about to finish this one. It's a little funny, but kind of boring. The main character sort of resembles you." She smiled at me.

"So I'm boring?" I laughed and she joined me. "Well, I was just checking on you, so I guess I'll go to my room." I turned to head to my room.

"Alright sweetie." I could hear her pick the book back up and turn a page.

It was surprising how my mom had changed so much.

When we came here, she was obsessed with herself and was always put together.

But now, she was always in sweats and had her hair thrown up on top of her head. And she always had a book. I didn't even know my mom knew how to read.

I went into my room and shut the door behind me.

I looked out my window and my dad was already outside again, working.

I wonder when he will leave. I loved having my dad here, but he was one more person I had to deal with.

I sat on my bed and laid down.

Alright, so Chase hated me and I had to see Adam everyday after school, alone.

What had Chase meant by Adam being 'no good for me'? Did Adam have something wrong with him or did he have a little secret? Which reminded me, what was Chase's dirty little secret? He could easily have any girl in the school, so why did he blackmail me?

I had no idea why I was so worried about it, because Chase and I were no longer dating or I guess, friends.

But should I try to get Chase and Adam talking again? Maybe tomorrow I could talk to Chase...

But Chase didn't want to talk to me and he made that very clear, so I shouldn't bother him.

I wonder what the principal will give me as a punishment tomorrow. Maybe I could pull the dead brother card and get out of it. I could just imagine saying I was sad, but I was too embarrassed to say anything. Yeah, I think he would fall for that.

Tomorrow would be yet another day filled with lies.

13

As I was driving to school, I wondered what Mr. Morris would say about my ditching. I figured he would just pull out the pity card and let it slide, but on second thought, he could completely go crazy and suspend me like he did with Adam.

I pulled into the very full parking lot. I glanced at the clock on the dashboard. I wasn't late, but I wasn't early.

I parked in the farthest spot imaginable. I got out and walked slowly to the building.

When I opened the door to the office, Mrs. Moore looked like she was expecting me.

"Well, hello Ms. Finely. Mr. Morris is waiting for you." She gestured with her hand to his office where I could see Mr. Morris reading a piece of paper.

I nodded at her and began making my way towards his office.

I stood in the doorway, afraid of what was next.

Mr. Morris must have heard Mrs. Moore's greeting because he was already looking up at me before I could even say his name.

"Ms. Finely," he nodded, "why don't you have a seat?" he asked.

I eyed the two intimidating chairs in front of his desk. I sat in the one closet to the door, preparing to get out of there as fast as I could.

"Alright, Scarlett, why don't you tell me why you skipped your last three classes?"

I tapped my foot on the floor nervously. I looked down at my hands, afraid to make eye contact with him. They always say you can tell if someone if lying by their eyes.

"Uh, I'm sorry Mr. Morris, I was just really sad and I didn't even think to come to your office before I left," I murmured.

I looked up at him and he looked like he had expected this answer.

"Well, yes," he sat up straight in his chair, "you should have told me. I would have let you go without a moment's hesitation Scarlett."

"I'm so sorry Mr. Morris," I said with no expression on my face.

"I guess I'll let you go with a warning. Just please don't skip school again Scarlett because I actually like you," he laughed.

"Thanks," I said with a smile.

"Well, you can go, but I want that sheet by the end of school today."

What sheet? Oh yeah, the one where you need to get the teacher's signatures. I think I shoved that into one of my books, but which book?

I got up from the chair and walked at a faster speed then normal. I looked at the clock on the wall above the door. It said 8:05, so I needed to run to my locker.

I opened the door and I started to run to the other building.

As I was running I could see everyone staring at me. I must look absolutely ridiculous running to school. Who runs to school?

"Ouch!" someone yelled.

I looked down and saw that I had knocked someone down.

He was big, so how did I not feel that?

"Oh my gosh! I'm so sorry!" I threw my hand over my mouth, shocked.

"It's alright, but could you help me up?" he asked while putting his hand out.

I grabbed his hand and tried to pull him up. I knew I wasn't much help, but I felt so bad.

Once he was up I got a good look at him. Wow, he was very, very good looking. Was anyone at this school not hot? His dark brown hair was a mess on the top of his head, but he pulled it off. He wore a light blue shirt with jeans; clearly he was new.

"Seriously, I'm really sorry, I'm running late," I said with a smile.

He smiled back and...wow. His bright white teeth almost blinded me, but I noticed he didn't have cute dimples like Chase.

"It's okay." He laughed. He held out his hand; yes, he was definitely new, "I'm Sebastian."

I shook his hand, "Hi, I'm Scarlett. You're new, right?" I asked.

He laughed, "How did you know?"

I eyed his jeans again, "the jeans. I wore jeans on my first day and I was stared at the whole time."

"I knew I shouldn't have worn jeans, but I didn't know what else to wear. You don't wear shorts a lot in Nebraska."

"Nebraska? You're a long way from home," I laughed.

"Yeah, definitely. And where are you from?" he asked.

"Everywhere," I answered.

He eyed me in confusion, "Everywhere?"

Just then, I remembered that I was running late.

"Uh, I really got to go. I guess I'll see you later Sebastian."

Before he could answer I was back to running.

When I finally got to my locker I was out of breath and probably a bit sweaty. Great, I just keep getting better and better.

I grabbed my Algebra II book quickly and I made my way to Mr. Rainer's class.

I wondered where Elaine was today. Normally she would be at my locker, waiting for me.

I walked into Mr. Rainer's class where Elaine sat perfectly still. I smiled at her and she smiled back with a bit more enthusiasm than normal.

I took my seat quickly and I glanced around the classroom where everyone was sitting perfectly still. What was up with everyone?

"Alright, let's begin," an unfamiliar voice announced.

I looked over to Mr. Rainer's desk and saw a tiny woman sitting in his chair staring at everyone.

She got up and walked to the dry erase board. "Your assignment is to do this page," she tapped her finger on the assignment that had been written on the board. "And you must show all of your work."

She said all of this without a smile. "And don't talk, or you will go see Mr. Morris."

Ah, so this must be why everyone was acting on their best behavior; they knew this lady would stick to her word and not let anyone make a peep.

I opened my book and began working; I didn't need to get into anymore trouble even if it meant I had to sit through this whole hour working on mind numbing Algebra.

When the bell rang, I let out a breath of relief. Everyone seemed as relieved as I was that this class was over.

I gathered my things and ran out of Mr. Rainer's classroom.

At my locker, was Elaine.

"Hey Scarlett! That class was terrible right? I wanted to give you a warning about Ms. Warran, but I didn't want to get into trouble." She finally stopped to catch her breath.

"Hey Elaine and its okay." I smiled at her.

We stood there in silence after I had made the exchange from my Algebra II book to my Junior English book.

"Alright, I guess I'll see you at lunch?" Elaine said it like a question.

"Of course." I smiled again.

She walked away and I made my way towards Mrs. Eisner's class.

Elaine was a great friend so I was going to be as nice as possible to her. But she seemed like she was in a great mood, but for no reason, I guess. I don't know what I'll do next year when she is gone and I'll have no one because at this rate, everyone I liked was leaving me.

Before I got to Mrs. Eisner's class, I stopped to calm myself. I hadn't seen Chase since yesterday and now I had to sit almost right next to him.

When I got into the classroom I scanned the desks for mine, but I couldn't find it.

I now realized why I couldn't; someone was already sitting at my desk.

Behind the person, though, was an empty spot. I contemplated taking this spot because it was right next to Chase.

I walked slowly to my desk. I immediately recognized the desk taker.

"Since you're new, I guess I'll let this one slide," I said to Sebastian.

He looked up at me and smiled. "And what is this that you are letting go?"

"You are in my spot," I said matter of factly.

"Oh, sorry, I didn't know this spot was taken. All of the ones in the back are taken so I just took the first one I could find," he explained.

"Like I said, you're new, so I'll let it slide."

He laughed and I joined him. "Well, I'm glad. Would you like me to move?" he asked.

"Uh, no, its fine. I'll just take the one behind you and secretly put sticky notes all over your back," I said with a wink.

Apparently, I was winking these days.

He started to chuckle and I took the spot behind him.

I looked to my left and saw Chase looking down at his desk. His cheeks were flushed and I now felt bad for flirting with Sebastian in front of him.

"Class, it seems we have another new student," Mrs. Eisner said after the bell rang.

She walked over to Sebastian's desk, "this is Sebastian Brody."

Sebastian kept his head forward, probably starting to hate Mrs. Eisner as much as I did.

She didn't introduce me on my first day unless you call the little lecture she had given to me on 'um' is considered one.

Mrs. Eisner turned around and walked back to her desk. "Open your books to page 45."

I guess it will be another day of listening to her lectures, waiting for it to end.

During the whole class, I kept my eyes on Sebastian's muscular back. He seemed like he was bigger than Chase and Adam combined.

I could see Chase look at me every once in a while.

I wanted him to know that he didn't need to worry about me liking Sebastian, but I had a feeling he wasn't worried, but more mad. Mad about what, I didn't know.

RRRRRIIIIINNNNGGGG!!! The bell's loud ring finally went off.

I literally jumped out of my seat so no one could stop me to talk.

I had a feeling I just made a new friend at Doven High, but I wasn't sure if I was too happy about it.

* * *

I walked into the cafeteria where Elaine was waiting for me at an empty table.

She waved enthusiastically, but I just smiled at her.

I waited in the long, slow line to get my food, though I didn't have an appetite.

"Hey Scarlett," Elaine said after I had sat down with my slice of pizza and water.

"Hey Elaine."

"So guess what?" Elaine asked.

This was what I waiting for, the reason she was in such a good mood.

"What?" I asked, bored.

"This guy at my work asked me out on a date last night!" she screamed.

"Oh really, where do you work?" I asked the least important question.

"At Hutton's; it's a restaurant down by the dock," she explained.

"Oh cool, so when are you going out?" I asked.

"Friday, so you have to come over sometime this week to help me pick out an outfit."

"I would love too, but I can't. I'm grounded and also I don't think you want my input on fashion," I laughed at my own joke.

"Why are you grounded?" Elaine asked.

Yep, just backed myself into a corner.

"Um...er...I kind of skipped classes after lunch yesterday?" I said.

She gasped with shock. "Why would you do that? Did you get into trouble with the principal?"

"Uh, I was just sad," that was all I was going to give her on the explanation, "and the principal let it slide."

"Oh, sad about your brother?" she asked.

"Yeah, about my brother," I lied, "so, I'm sorry I can't help you with the outfit, but call me on Saturday and tell me all about it!" I tried to change the subject.

"Definitely," she smiled.

We sat in silence for a couple of minutes.

"So did you see the new kid? He is really hot," Elaine exclaimed.

"Yeah, his name is Sebastian," I said.

"Oh, do you have any classes with him?"

"Yeah, Junior English and I ran into him today before school. That's how I met him," I laughed.

Elaine giggled.

"How could you knock him down? He is so big!" she said.

I wondered the same thing. "Um, I don't really know," I laughed.

"Well, I have to go to the library today," Elaine started to get up, "so I guess I'll see you later."

"Yeah, see you later," I said.

I watched her dump her food and make her way towards the library.

That used to be me and now here I was, sitting by myself at the lunch table.

"Red head sure has a mouth," Sebastian said after he sat by me.

"What?" I asked confused.

"I was going to sit next to you when she left, if she was going to leave. But it just looked like she was going to talk forever."

"Yeah, Elaine sure is a talker," I said with a laugh.

"So, I asked about a dozen people and I had no sticky notes on my back," Sebastian said.

I shrugged my shoulders. "Mrs. Eisner was staring at you the whole time, so I didn't want to take the risk."

"Yeah, is that normal for her to stare like that?" he asked.

"She stared at me for the first couple of days, so I would expect some more tomorrow, if I were you."

"When did you move here?" he wondered.

"I started here about three weeks ago, but technically I haven't even gone to this school for a week" I murmured.

He looked at me, confused. "What do you mean?"

"I was gone for the past two weeks and the first week I was only here for about three days, I think," I explained.

RRRRRRRIIIIIIINNNNGGGG!!! The bell rang loudly.

I started to get up and dump my untouched food.

Sebastian followed me. "It seems like every time I want an answer out of you, you have to run off," he chuckled.

"Yeah, I guess life just works that way. So where are you headed?"

We started to walk out of the cafeteria and to the direction of my locker.

"Algebra II with Rainer. Do you know it?" he asked.

"Yeah, I have that first hour. But Mr. Rainer isn't here, so beware of the substitute."

"Not a nice gal?" he asked.

"I think her exact words were 'talk and I send you to the principal's office.'" I giggled.

"Alright, thanks for the heads up. So I guess I'll see you later," Sebastian said.

"Yeah, later." I smiled.

After he was gone, I looked around and saw everyone staring at me.

What was with the staring? Was it because I was talking to the new guy?

I could feel myself smiling.

I immediately composed my face.

I was just flirting, that's all.

I will not fall for another guy here, I thought to myself before heading off to my next class.

14

Alright, one more class. I've gotten all of my signatures, except for Mr. Tilden's.

"Hi Mr. Tilden," I greeted the small man.

"Ah, hello Ms. Scarlett Finely. I hope you are better." He smiled.

I got out my homework, though there was not much. "Yeah, I'm fine, but Mr. Morris said that you need to sign this paper," I handed him the yellow paper, "showing that I've given you all the homework from when I was gone."

"Well of course," he said. He quickly scribbled his name and handed the paper back to me.

"Thanks and also I just wanted to let you know that I'm going to meet up with Adam to work on the project, so no worries."

"It sounds like you have everything handled Scarlett," Mr. Tilden said.

He had never said my first name by itself.

I turned around and headed for my seat.

"You know, I would say you're a stalker, but I think that's a little harsh."

I turned to see Sebastian sitting in Adam's desk.

"Yeah, I think that would be a bit harsh," I told him.

"Alright, so what's the news with this guy? He greeted me like he was from a different century. Is that normal?" Sebastian asked.

I laughed, but then quickly composed myself because people were starting to look at me rather than Sebastian.

"Uh, yeah, that's very normal. That's actually how he greeted me on my first day," I explained.

He looked relieved. "Okay, good because after Ms. Warran, I thought I had no hope at this school," he laughed.

"I told you. I actually worked on homework in that class because I didn't want to go see the principal."

We laughed in unison.

The bell rang and Sebastian turned to the front, but Mr. Tilden still looked busy.

"Oh yeah, I forgot to tell you, that desk is taken, too," I whispered to Sebastian.

He turned his head, perplexed. "And who does this desk belong to?"

"Adam Wilson. He was suspended, but he'll be back."

"Oh, I don't doubt that," he laughed, "I guess I won't have to worry until he comes back."

"Yeah, I guess not."

Mr. Tilden cleared his throat, but he was still looking down at his desk.

He suddenly snapped his neck up and he looked at Sebastian. This was followed with a smile.

"Uh oh, here we go," I said under my breath.

"Mr. Sebastian Brody, welcome to Doven High!" Mr. Tilden said enthusiastically.

"Um, thanks," Sebastian mumbled.

"Why don't you tell us where you are from?" Mr. Tilden asked.

I felt so sorry for Sebastian because I actually knew how he felt.

"Nebraska." Short and quick. He must have wanted this over as soon as possible.

"Ah, interesting." Was all Mr. Tilden said.

He turned around and walked back over to his desk.

After a couple of minutes of head nodding, Mr. Tilden talked again.

"Well Mr. Brody, we are in the middle of a project right now, so I guess you're off the hook unless you want to join a group or do it by yourself?"

Sebastian turned his head and looked at me. I shrugged my shoulders.

"Uh, I think I'll pass Mr. Tilden, but thanks," Sebastian said politely.

"That's what I thought," Mr. Tilden laughed.

"Good response," I mouthed to Sebastian.

"Thanks," he mouthed back.

"Alright, children, I guess you can work on your projects with your partners," Mr. Tilden said.

Everyone moved around to sit by their partners and then the murmur of voices began.

Sebastian turned to me, "so why aren't you moving to find your partner?"

"Like I said, suspended," I said.

"Ah, I see."

"Yeah, so why don't you tell me why you moved?" I asked.

"My dad got a new job," he said.

I nodded my head showing that I understood.

"Which brings me to my question, why are you here?" he asked.

"My mom and I just move around a lot, that's all." That was all that was going to be said on the subject if I had anything to say about it.

"You guys just move for no reason?" Sebastian asked in confusion. Clearly he wasn't getting that I did not want to talk about this at all.

"Yeah, pretty much." I turned in my chair so I was looking forward. I was trying to indicate I was done talking, but Sebastian was still turned waiting for more of an answer; something he was not going to get.

"Huh," was all he said before he turned in his desk to face forward.

I was just starting to like this kid, but he clearly didn't like my answers and I knew tomorrow I would have more questions thrown at me. Should I lie? Or should I just tell him the truth? But he didn't know my past, so why tell him? I knew he would probably look at my differently after I told him; something I didn't want. I was actually normal to this kid and that's how it was going to stay.

I glanced out the window and saw that nothing had changed in the parking lot, but why should it have?

Clearly, I needed something to distract me so I wasn't thinking so much.

I got up and walked over to Mr. Tilden's desk. What was I doing exactly?

He looked up and smiled. "Yes, Ms. Finely?" he asked.

"Uh," I looked down at my hands nervously, "I just wanted to apologize for how Adam treated you." Why was I apologizing for Adam? I certainly didn't need too, but for some reason I felt this was my fault.

"Oh, well, you don't need to apologize Scarlett. It was not your fault," Mr. Tilden said.

"I know, but I just want to apologize," I smiled.

"Well, thank you Ms. Finely," he smiled back.

I started to walk back to my desk, but Mr. Tilden stopped me.

"Scarlett, considering the circumstances, if you want a new partner, you can change, if you want."

"No, that's okay Mr. Tilden."

"Oh, well would you at least like some more time?"

More time? Sure I needed more time, but not for the project. I needed more time to prepare to see Adam today. I needed more time to prepare my answers for Sebastian. And I needed more time to talk to Chase.

"No, that's okay Mr. Tilden. I'll take what I've got."

"Oh, well alright Ms. Finely, but just let me know."

I turned and walked back to my seat. When I finally sat down, I could feel Sebastian staring at me.

"So why were you gone for 2 weeks?" Sebastian asked.

Yeah, I definitely needed more time.

* * *

I pulled into his driveway and turned off my car.

I took a deep breath and did some breathing exercises I learned from my mom.

Alright, just an hour, you can do it, I thought.

As I got out of the car I thought about what I had told Sebastian. I simply told him that my brother had died and I needed time to grieve. He hadn't given me the head tilt or even the face he just said that was 'too bad' and then proceeded to stare at the dry erase board for the rest of class.

I knocked on his door and waited impatiently for him to answer it.

The door swung open and Adam was standing there with wet hair and no shirt on.

"You could at least put a shirt on," I said while walking by him and into the house.

He chuckled, "I was just getting out of the shower."

"I told you I would be here after school so maybe you should take your showers earlier."

I didn't know why I was being so snappy, but that was the only way I could keep my guard up around him.

"Jeez, what's with the 'tud?" he asked.

"I don't know what you're talking about, but we should get started." I got out the books I had checked out from the library during my free period.

I handed him the thinnest one.

"Thanks," he mumbled.

"I figured I would do the later years and you could do the earlier years. Does that sound okay?" I asked even though I didn't really care what he thought about it.

"Yeah, sure," he said.

For the first fifteen minutes I worked hard and got a lot of notes taken, but when I had glanced up to make sure he was working, he was staring at me.

"Yes, can I help you?" I asked rudely.

"I like that shirt," he pointed to the yellow blouse I had thrown on this morning.

"Uh, thanks," I could feel my face flush, "but I think maybe you should concentrate more on the project."

After that, I was too worried that he staring at me so I didn't get much work done.

I looked up and saw that he had a bunch of notes written down. I was surprised, but some how I knew Adam was smart and that he just didn't apply his self.

When the hour mark was up, I remembered something very important.

"OH NO!" I gasped.

I jumped up and ran to the phone.

"What?" Adam ran after me.

I dialed the number quickly and waited impatiently for someone to answer.

"Hello?" my dad asked, worried. He must have been waiting for my call.

"Dad! I'm so sorry! I totally forgot to call you! I'm about to leave so I'll be home in a few minutes," I said before he could interrupt me.

"Alright, I'll see you then," he said sternly.

At that moment I could here the line cut out. Yeah, he was really mad.

I hung up the phone and ran to gather my stuff.

"Alright, I'll see you tomorrow at the same time, so let's wear a shirt this time," I said while making my way towards the door.

Adam laughed again, loudly. "Okay, I'll see you tomorrow Scarlett."

I closed the door behind me and ran to my car. I was going to be in so much trouble when I got home and I knew it.

As I drove home I wondered what punishment my dad would think of. He could ban me from Adam's altogether, but it was school related, so I doubt he would do that.

I was probably going to get the silent treatment or something crazy like that to show he was mad at me and that I would not be soon forgiven.

I parked my car in my driveway and walked up to my house.

Alright, here we go. I opened the door, but my dad wasn't waiting for me in the kitchen like I had expected.

"In here Scarlett!" my dad yelled.

I walked ominously around the house looking for my dad's angry face.

I finally found him in the living room, watching TV. My mom was sitting in the chair next to him, sleeping.

"I'm so sorry dad. I'll call tomorrow, I swear," I whispered.

He nodded. "I decided I wasn't going to be mad at you. But just please, please call me from now on, okay? I was really worried."

"Scout's honor," I held up my hand like I was giving an oath.

My dad chuckled quietly, but returned his focus back on the TV.

I turned and walked to the kitchen. What was with that? He didn't punish me at all, but why not? Was it just because my mom was right there and would he give me the real punishment later?

I grabbed water from the refrigerator and then I ran up to my room.

I closed the door behind me and sat on my bed.

Maybe things were starting to look up.

15

"Hey Scarlett!" Elaine yelled while approaching my locker.

I turned to greet her, but I paused to take a look at her outfit today. She was wearing daisy duke style shorts, bright pink cowboy boots, and a sleeveless flannel shirt. It looked like there was a stain on the collar of the shirt, but the boots were spotless.

"Hey Elaine, going to a rodeo today?" I laughed.

She looked at me confused and that's when I realized that she must have really liked this outfit for just casual wear. "What?" she asked.

"Um, nothing," I lied. Did she always dress like this? Maybe I didn't pay enough attention to her to see what her outfits consisted of. That was going to be put on my list: pay more attention to Elaine.

"Oh okay," she sighed. "So are you ready for Algebra today?"

"Ms. Warran isn't here today, is she?" I cringed.

"No, Mr. Rainer is back," she laughed.

I let out of breath of relief, "okay, good because I didn't really feel like sitting like a statue this morning."

We laughed in unison.

"Alright, I guess we should go to class," Elaine said after we had caught our breath from laughing so hard.

I grabbed my Algebra II book and we headed off to Mr. Rainer's room.

When we got in there, Mr. Rainer was sitting behind his desk, bewildered. He must be regretting taking yesterday off because I could see a pile of papers at the corner of his desk saying 'GRADE.' He had a long night ahead of him.

I walked to my desk slowly; today I was oddly early to school.

I sat down and noticed no one was in the room besides a girl with short brown hair, a guy with pink streaks in his hair, Elaine, and me. I glanced up at the clock - it said 8:05, so I was only five minutes early. I can kill five minutes no problem.

I got out my math book and looked over my homework that I had done for today. It was the first time I actually had finished it and most importantly, understood it.

I checked every answer and I looked over all my work to make sure it matched my answer.

After I had finished doing my checking, I glanced up at the clock and realized it was now 8:10.

RRRRRRRRIIIIIIIINNNNNNGGGGG!!!!

School was ready to begin.

Students started to pile into the small classroom and make their way to their desks. I noticed one girl had mascara streaming down her face and the one behind her looked pissed; clearly a fight had occurred.

I could hear papers shuffling and students preparing for this wretched class.

"Alright, class, sorry I was gone. I hope you weren't much of a hassle for Ms. Warran. She didn't leave any notes, so I'm guessing you were all perfect angels." He smiled.

After Mr. Rainer's greeting, I completely shut out the lesson.

I doodled on a piece of paper and I analyzed everyone in the class.

The girl sitting in front of me had a massive case of dandruff and she was wearing a black shirt, which made matters worse. Her fingernails were painted the darkest red I could imagine before it transformed into a different shade. When I noticed how nice her nails looked, I looked down at my hands. My nails were so short because I chewed on them whenever I was nervous and then I realized my fingers were really long and bony.

After that I stopped looking at the girl in front of me and turned to stare at the guy who was diagonal from me. His bright red hair was buzzed and freckles seemed to cover every inch of his body. His ears were smaller than average.

Self consciously I had grabbed one of my ears. It seemed normal sized, so I didn't worry.

Finally, after I had analyzed everyone else, I looked at what I was wearing.

I was wearing a dark green v-neck shirt that I had grabbed from the dryer this morning. My khaki shorts were a little shorter than I liked, but they didn't look bad or at least I didn't think they looked bad. My hair was a mess this morning so I threw it up in a pony tail.

At that point, the bell rang so I gathered my stuff quickly and went to my locker to make my book exchange.

To my surprise, Elaine didn't meet me there.

I shut my locker which I now realized barely closed, and I headed off to Mrs. Eisner's class.

Just like yesterday, Sebastian was in my seat.

"Alright, I guess I can let it slide again," I joked. I sat down in my seat and he turned to talk to me.

"Well, you did say that you would sit there so you could put things on my back, but you didn't get too yesterday, so I figured I would give you another chance today." He smiled.

"Oh, well, in that case..." I laughed.

"Sebastian, turn around and Scarlett, do not distract him," Mrs. Eisner demanded.

Sebastian obediently turned around and I could hear his quiet chuckle.

I must not have heard the bell because Mrs. Eisner decided to go on with the lesson. Just like last hour, I blocked the teacher out.

Instead of analyzing everyone; I just doodled on a piece of paper.

I could feel Chase glance at my every once in a while and I would shift in my chair so he could see less and less of my face.

When class was finally over, I noticed Sebastian was lingering at the door.

"Wanted to get some alone time with Mrs. Eisner?" I joked.

He chuckled. "No, actually, I was waiting for you."

Why was he waiting for me? Were we friends now? "Oh, well aren't you a gentleman," I said.

We started to walk in the general direction of my locker.

"Yeah, I suppose," he said with a smile.

I grabbed my Biology II book and shut my locker.

All of a sudden, Sebastian grabbed my books.

"Can I help you?" I asked, confused.

"A gentleman always carries books for a lady." He winked.

We walked in silence to Ms. Garrett's room. Sebastian smelled a lot like Adam, like a field of flowers. I couldn't help but sneak a few peeks at him while we walked slowly.

Once we made it to the doorway, we stopped.

"Alright, I guess this is where we part," he joked. He handed me my books, one by one.

"Alright, thanks," I said.

He smiled and then turned and walked away.

I definitely, definitely, definitely can't fall for yet another guy here at Doven High.

* * *

"Alright, I think I have picked out the perfect outfit for Friday," Elaine ranted.

Today I had gotten to the table first so I impatiently waited for my table mate so I didn't look so lonely, which I sort of was.

"Oh that's great, so what does the ensemble look like?" I asked enthusiastically. I needed to keep as many friends as I could. And by experience, being a quiet, moody person is not one way to befriend someone.

"I'm going to wear like these really cute skinny jeans that are super dark. I mean I'm talking almost black here, but they aren't black. But anyways, my shirt is like this pale pink with ruffles on the front," she gestured her hand to her chest. "And its so cute! Oh my gosh, I wish you weren't grounded so you could see it!"

By last night's encounter with my dad, it didn't really seem like I was grounded. Why did he act so calmly about me not calling when he specifically told me too? I was expecting World War III or something, but instead he was totally Zen about it. Something was definitely wrong and I wanted to know what was up.

"Scarlett?" Elaine shook my arm.

Back to the present. "Oh, sorry Elaine," I apologized.

"You've been spacing out a lot lately, is something wrong?" With these words came both the head tilt and the face. Oh how I hated the face.

"Oh, I'm fine, I just have a lot on my mind," I said.

"Oh, alright, but you can tell me if there was something wrong," she said with a smile.

She was too nice. "Thanks, Elaine."

For the rest of lunch, we sat in silence and nibbled on our sandwiches.

Lately, I was never hungry. My dad just said it was because I was sad, but I had a feeling that wasn't the reason.

* * *

I walked into Mr. Tilden's class quickly because I was running late.

After my last hour, I realized I had to pee badly so I ran to the bathroom while ignoring all the points and stares.

After I had finished in the bathroom, I headed towards my locker.

While I was pulling out my history book, though, the bell rang.

I looked around me and saw no one in the hall except for the janitor.

Now, I was preparing for a detention as I walked in the small room with bright white walls that had been covered with posters from every era.

"Ah, Ms. Finely, I didn't think you were the tardy kind," Mr. Tilden said as I approached his desk.

"I'm really sorry Mr. Tilden, I just had to…"

"No excuses Scarlett," Mr. Tilden interrupted.

I looked around the class, but no one was staring at me, thank the lord.

"Should I give you a detention or some other form of punishment?" Mr. Tilden contemplated.

I waited for my punishment, quietly. I didn't really think my dad would get mad about it because I wasn't planning on telling him.

"Ok, I'll be Mr. Nice Guy today, but only today. No punishment Ms. Scarlett," Mr. Tilden decided.

I let out a breath of relief, "thanks Mr. Tilden," I said graciously.

I skipped to my desk and sat down.

"Tardy hardy?" Sebastian joked.

I turned to look at him. "This is the first time, so don't you be making assumptions about me."

We laughed, but then were cut off short by Mr. Tilden clearing his throat.

"Class, you can just work on your projects today, I have some work I need to catch up on."

Everyone started to get up and mingle with their partners and other students.

Sebastian and I were still facing each other. "So, how is your project coming along?" Sebastian asked.

"Well, we are getting some done, but I have a feeling it won't be A+ plus work," I said.

Even though both Adam and I had taken notes yesterday, I didn't think we had a chance at actually combining everything and putting it on a Power Point.

"Oh, well that's too bad," Sebastian said.

"Yeah, I guess," I smiled.

For the rest of class Sebastian and I joked about the pros and cons of moving to new towns.

"Alright, I guess I'll see you tomorrow," Sebastian said after he had walked me out to my car.

"Yeah, see you tomorrow." I turned my key to turn the car on, but the car was making no recognition that it was working.

I kept turning the key, but nothing was happening.

"What is wrong with my car?" I asked myself.

"I think your battery died," Sebastian said. I thought he had left, but apparently not.

"So what does that mean?" I asked. I had not one clue what a battery was doing in my car. I knew absolutely nothing about cars.

"Its means, your car isn't going to be going anywhere," Sebastian chuckled.

"I don't think it's very funny," I snapped.

Sebastian abruptly stopped, "sorry."

"Its okay, but I hate to ask…"

"Do you need a ride?" he finished my thought.

"Yes, please," I begged. For some reason, just because I had met Sebastian yesterday, I felt that it was safe for me to take a ride from him.

He opened the door for me, "alright, let's go."

I grabbed my book bag and locked the car.

We headed towards Sebastian's car, which felt like it was a mile away.

"Did you really have to park so far away?" I joked once we got to his little pickup truck.

"I was one of the last ones here, which means you park the farthest away," he laughed.

He unlocked the car and I jumped in. The inside of his truck was a mess, with crumpled papers all over.

"Sorry 'bout the mess," he apologized after he saw me eyeing the wrappers under my feet.

"It's okay," I said.

He started his truck and unlike my car, it roared to life.

He turned to look at me. "Alright, where to Scarlett?"

16

"Nice house," Sebastian said after he had parked in the slant-like driveway.

"Uh, it's not mine," I said, embarrassed.

"Oh yeah? Whose is it then?" he wondered.

I started to gather all of my things onto my lap so I could get out of this truck as fast as I could. "Adam Wilson's," I muttered.

I looked up to see his facial expression, but I was surprised to see him confused. "Who is Adam?" he asked.

"The kid who got suspended," his facial expression didn't change so I decided to continue with my profile of Adam. "You sit in his seat in history. You know, my history partner?"

He nodded his head like he understood. "Ah, okay, I know who you are talking about, kind of, considering I've never met the guy," he laughed.

I started to open the door, but then remembered something very vital.

"Sebastian, I hate to ask, but could you pick me up in like an hour?" My mom would have told me I was being very rude, asking someone to drive me places even though I just met them, but mom had changed, much like I had.

Sebastian looked out the window, and then his eyes glanced at the clock on his dashboard.

"Uh, sure, no problem. I'll see in you an hour," he finished with a smile.

"Thanks, I owe you." I opened the door and shut it as soft as I could behind me.

I could hear Sebastian's truck as it hit the curb while he backed out of the driveway.

I wanted to turn to wave, but I was afraid he would have seen my blush. I was asking too much of this guy and I had to figure out a way to repay him. Maybe I would get him candy or something. But that seems childish.

I could just imagine his laugh as I handed him a box of chocolates. "Thanks, I really appreciate the ride," I would say, feeling the heat from my blush on my face. And from then on, Sebastian would see me as a child and mock me for my sugary ways.

Ah, the misery it would cause me.

I knocked on Adam's door and then followed it with repeatedly pushing the door bell.

Be as mean as you can, I told myself.

When he opened the door, a wide grin was covering his face.

"Well, at least you wore a shirt," I said as I pushed him aside to get inside.

I could hear his booming laugh as I made my way towards the kitchen.

I grabbed his phone and quickly dialed my home number.

"You don't mind if I use your phone, right?" I asked Adam as I waited for my dad to answer.

"I don't really care," he murmured.

"Hello?" my dad answered.

"Hey dad, I'm just letting you know I made it to Adam's house," I said.

"Oh okay, thanks kid. I'll see you in a hour, right?" he asked. He sounded like he was preoccupied.

"Yeah, but dad…" I began.

"Alright, 'bye kid," my dad cut me off. Immediately, I heard the dial tone.

Wow, that was rude, I thought. I hung up Adam's phone and turned to look at him.

"But what?" he asked.

"What?" I asked confused.

"You said 'yeah, but dad' so what were you going to tell him?" he asked while taking a bite of an apple.

"Well, I guess you're an eavesdropper these days," I said with a smile.

"Hey, you used my phone. I can listen to whatever you say." He winked.

"I was going to tell him that I got here, but my car didn't." I could feel my face flush.

I turned and walked to the couch that I had sat on yesterday. I could hear Adam's loud footsteps behind me. "What does that mean? Did your car break down? How did you get here?"

I really didn't want to answer the last question because I really didn't want to tell Adam about Sebastian. Even though Adam wasn't my boyfriend, I would still feel guilty as I watched his face while I talked about getting a ride from another guy. I would get that gut wrenching pain that usually bothered me when I lied to anyone.

"Uh, yeah, my car broke down," I muttered. That was all I was going to give him, though I knew his next question...

"And how did you get here?" I wasn't looking at his face because I didn't want to be distracted, but I could hear him take a bite from the apple, chew, and then swallow.

I cleared my throat and I looked at his face, gut reaction.

"Uh, well, there is this new kid at school?" I said it like a question. "And he offered to give me a ride, so I took it." I watched his face, but it didn't change at all.

"Why would you take a ride from a complete stranger? Haven't you ever heard of 'stranger danger?'" he did air quotes.

"Well, he seemed nice, so I didn't feel like there was any risk."

"Yeah, that's how they get their prey, Scarlett. They act like the nice guy and then BAM! You are dead and buried in an abandoned field. You need to seriously watch the news," he started to laugh because he must have been amusing his self.

"Thanks for the heads up dad, but I think I'll be okay," I joked.

As soon as I said this, though, Adam's face dropped.

"Seriously Scarlett, be more careful, please." Crunch, chew, and swallow.

Fifty minutes later, I was gathering all of the notes I had taken. Today I was pretty productive, I almost finished the note taking on more than half of the era. I glanced over to Adam's notebook which was also filled with notes. Well, he was making progress at least.

"Okay, I'll see you tomorrow Adam," I said I made my way towards the front door.

He followed me. "Wait, how are you getting home? Do you want me to give you a ride?" he asked.

I contemplated telling him the truth, but then decided to tell him that Sebastian was taking me home because he would inevitably see Sebastian's truck in the driveway.

"The new kid is taking me home, but thanks anyways," I said quickly.

"No," Adam said.

I looked up at him and his face was completely serious. "What?" I asked, surprised. Who was he, to tell me who I can and can't get a ride from?

"You barely know the guy," Adam said angrily.

"His name is Sebastian," I defended.

"I don't really care what the hell his name is Scarlett. Now come on, I'll give you a ride." He started to put his shoes on, but then I heard Sebastian's honk.

"He is already here Adam and I'm not going to be rude. So, I'll see you tomorrow, okay?" I asked, but I didn't wait for an answer.

I opened the door and slammed it behind me.

Adam shouldn't tell me what to do. He shouldn't be mad – he had no right.

I opened the door to Sebastian's truck and jumped into the passenger's seat.

"Sorry, I would have been out here earlier, but Adam was having a little fit," I joked. I started to laugh, but then soon realized Sebastian wasn't laughing with me.

He wasn't even looking at me. I looked to see what he was glaring at.

Sure enough, Adam was making his way towards Sebastian's truck.

"You've got to be kidding me," I muttered under my breath.

Adam started to walk to my side and I could feel Sebastian's eyes staring at me. I turned my head to give him an apologetic look, but then jumped after Adam had knocked on the window, loudly.

I rolled down the window quickly. I just wanted this over with.

"Here," Adam said while throwing a notebook at me.

"What's this?" I asked. I didn't recognize the cover.

"It's my notebook. I took a lot of notes last night and then finished today. I figured I would give it to you, so you didn't have to worry about coming back here." He shot a glance at Sebastian.

"Uh, okay? We're presenting the projects next week, so I'll just do the Power Point and then you'll be back by then, right?" I stammered.

"Yeah, I'll be back." This was clearly a warning.

Before I could say anything else, Adam was already walking back up the driveway, to his front door.

As we backed up, I watched Adam slam his front door.

He clearly had issues.

"I'm really sorry about that," I apologized to Sebastian.

"Its okay, I've had to deal with many ex girlfriends," he laughed.

"Oh, he isn't my ex," I said.

Sebastian looked at me, but then returned his focus to the road. "Could have fooled me."

* * *

After Sebastian dropped me off, dad and I headed over to the school to retrieve my car.

"Sebastian told me the battery is dead," I said, but then quickly regretted mentioning Sebastian. I didn't want my dad to get all nosy.

My dad was looking under the hood while I stood off to the side unaware of what I should do.

"Well, Sebastian is right," my dad said.

No questions about Sebastian? My dad was really starting to scare me a little.

In the past two days, I didn't even recognize the man. First, he didn't even care that I didn't call him and now he was just acting like having a bunch of guys in my life was completely normal.

After twenty minutes of my dad poking and prodding under the hood, the tow truck he had called showed up.

"Your car will be at the shop down on Garrison, so you can pick it up there when it's fixed," the driver explained as he got into the driver's side of his truck.

"Alright, thanks," my dad said with an appreciating nod.

The guy pulled out of the parking lot and followed him was a trail of smoke. Wow, he was definitely a polluter. I wondered how many people have given him lectures about global warming. I'm sure by now he just nodded rather than start a debate about recycling.

* * *

"What's for dinner?" I asked once my dad and I got home.

He threw his keys on the counter and started to make his way towards the couch he seemed to be living on. "I guess whatever you make yourself." He plopped down on the couch.

My mom was no where in site, so she must be in her room.

"How is mom today?" I asked cautiously. My mom's mental health was a sore subject.

"She seems good. You need to stop worrying about her Scarlett. She likes to read and that's keeping her distracted, so why push it?" He turned on the TV and started to flip through the channels.

I turned and walked to the kitchen.

I opened the refrigerator's door with hopes of finding something appetizing.

Nothing, as I had suspected.

I rummaged through the cabinets and found a bag of unopened chips. I grabbed a can of soda and ran up the stairs, to my room. Before I shut my door, though, I heard a noise.

It sounded like it was coming from my mom's room so I tiptoed to her door and pressed my ear to it.

I could hear a soft weeping.

I opened the door, but instead of my mom stopping to compose her self, she just continued to cry.

"Is the book sad?" I asked.

She grabbed a tissue and blew into it. "Yeah, the book is sad."

We both knew the truth.

I jumped onto her bed and opened the bag of chips.

I offered her some, with the expectations of her refusing, but she shoved her hand into the bag and pulled out her hand, full of chips.

For hours, mom and I just sat silently and ate the bag of chips.

It was time to face the facts; it was over here for mom and me.

17

"Moving? But why? You just got here," Elaine said, dumbfounded.

We were sitting at lunch, by ourselves, of course.

"It's just time. You know, a fresh start?" Why was I explaining myself?

Last night I told my mom that we tried to stay, but we just needed to leave. She agreed after I had taken a few more minutes of persuading her. Together, we went downstairs and told my dad of our plans. He too was happy. He told us that he thought it was best for him to move away from Washington and in with us.

Mom and I both looked at each other, surprised. After dad realized we were stunned he explained that he wasn't trying to get back together with mom, he just wanted us all to be a family again.

The only decision we had to make was where we were going to move.

Mom said somewhere sunny and dad suggested I should decide. They gave me two days to decide while they packed our possessions. Dad said he was just going to hire someone to move his stuff to wherever we decided to go.

"Well, I'm going to miss you." Elaine hugged me tight.

"Yeah, I'm really going to miss you too." I truly meant it. Elaine was the first 'real' friend I had. Sure, I had been friends with Casey, but for more than half of our relationship I was sleeping with her boyfriend, so I don't really think that counts.

For the rest of lunch, Elaine and I exchanged numbers and e-mail addresses.

Dad told me he would deal with the principal, so I didn't really have to worry about that.

Once I got to history, though, I decided it was best to warn Mr. Tilden.

"Mr. Tilden, I have something to tell you," I said.

He looked up from his computer screen, "Yes, Ms. Scarlett?"

"Uh, well, I'm moving and that means I can't do the project." I already had Adam's notebook in my hand to give to Mr. Tilden. I wasn't really sure if I was going to see Adam before I left.

"Oh, moving already? Well I'll miss you Ms. Finely," he said with a smile.

I handed him Adam's notebook, "This is Adam's. He gave it to me so I could set up the Power Point, but I don't think I will see him before I leave. I put my notes in there too, so he didn't have to do all the work."

Last night, I had gone through my notebook and ripped all the pages of my notes out. I shoved them into Adam's notebook. I then had written a letter telling him how I was moving and that I'm sorry for everything. I decided this would be my good-bye. He at least deserved that.

"Oh well, I will send this home with his homework." Mr. Tilden put it under a stack of papers labeled 'Adam Wilson.'

"Oh, when is that being sent to him?" Half of me wanted the note to get to him after I had left. I really didn't expect Adam to come and stop me; after all we barely knew each other. But the other half wanted him to get it before I had left, so he would try to stop me.

"Uh, tomorrow, I believe."

"Oh okay, thanks Mr. Tilden."

He turned his focus back to the computer so I suspected this was my time to leave.

"So, moving already?" Sebastian asked after I had settled into my desk.

"Yeah, its time." The same answer I gave to Elaine. The same answer I was going to give if anyone asked.

"I guess I will be all alone here at Doven High," he joked.

"Yeah, but you could always try to make friends," I laughed.

"Yeah, I'm not too great at that."

"What are you talking about? You befriended me," I pointed out.

"Is that what we are? Friends?" he asked.

I didn't really understand his question, but I hinted a double meaning.

"Of course," I smiled with a grin that touched my eyes.

"Alright, class, today we are going to talk about..." Mr. Tilden began his lecture.

The whole class I couldn't help but steal a couple of glances in Sebastian's direction.

He never turned to look at me; the thing he would normally do.

As I walked to my locker I couldn't help but realize this was my last Friday I'll ever have at Doven High.

Which brought me to my dilemma, where was I going to move?

Sunny was out. Maybe somewhere cold. Rain was definitely appreciated.

* * *

"Honey, is pizza okay for dinner?" my mom asked as I dropped my dad's car keys on the counter.

At this moment, my car was being worked on by a mechanic that was being paid too much for doing little. My dad agreed to let me borrow his rental car.

"Oh, that's fine." I smiled at my mom who seemed in a better mood, but stressed about packing. She was always like this when we moved. I've learned to ignore it because it would pass.

I grabbed a few empty boxes and walked up the stairs; I needed to pack if they wanted to be out of here by next week.

When I walked into my room, though, it was empty except for my bed and a pile of clothes that I suspected were for me to wear these next few days.

Well, that was nice of my parents, I thought.

I jumped on my mattress which was pushed up against the far wall next to the window.

I turned my head and looked out the window, noticing the sunset. For once in my life, I was noticing small details. For instance, if I smiled a certain way, I had one dimple. And my mom had a mole on the back of her neck while my dad had a freckle on his palm.

These little things would be here for as long as my parents and I were here. But, this particular sunset, would not. Tomorrow there might be more orange than red or yellow. Or the sun might be one inch over.

Why I was thinking all of this, I had no clue, but for some reason it seemed vital.

Everything changes in some sort of way.

My life has changed. My parents have clearly changed. And I, well I hardly recognized myself.

In the mirror, of course, I was the same Scarlett. The girl who always wore her hair long and her eye brows perfect. Her blue eyes were striking against her pale skin. And that one little dimple, made her look innocent.

But Scarlett, as a person, had changed.

When I first moved here I was quiet and just hoping for this life to be over with. I was still dwelling on my past and I couldn't focus on the future.

I wanted to make as little as friends as possible, but for some reason or another, I had made friends. Real friends. Elaine, I was going to keep contact with. Chase, not so much.

He obviously didn't want to talk to me, so why waste both time and energy on keeping contact with him?

Elaine, though, was a good friend. She was there every week after my brothers' passing. Even though she talked the whole time, it was just nice to feel someone's lively presence in the house.

And Adam, well, I had no idea what to do with Adam. He had barely taken a major role in my life, but in so many ways, he was the main act. He was the one who scooped me off the dock and he was the one who cooked me eggs and bacon for breakfast.

Adam, was the one.

The one what, I couldn't tell you. But he was definitely something.

I jumped up from my mattress – I clearly just had an epiphany.

I stumbled downstairs. My mom was next to the front door.

"Where are you going?" she asked.

"It's my turn, mom," I said while grabbing the keys to my dad's rental car. As I ran out the door I could hear her ask my turn for what.

I had no time to explain to her what I was doing. There was no time to waste.

I started the car, which purred to life. I backed out of the driveway too fast for comfort.

As I sped down the road, I finally had my answer for my mom.

It was my turn to fall in love, just like she had done in all of my other 'homes.' It was my turn to find a home away from home. It was my turn to speak my mind.

After a short five minutes, I was in the neighborhood that had become familiar to me. 708, turn head, and there was 709.

The lights were on, indicating someone was home. Let's just hope it's the someone I'm looking for.

I parked into the slant-like driveway, but kept the car running; I had no idea what the outcome of this little endeavor would be.

I pounded on the door, soon realizing I was no hulk. I rubbed my hand, trying to dissolve the pain for the time being.

"Scarlett? What are you doing here?" Adam asked. He was once again shirtless. Why did he do this to me?

"I don't want to move," I declared.

"You're moving?" he asked, dumbfounded.

"My parents are packing the house right now."

"But why?"

"I told them I wanted to move." My face flushed. I looked down at my hand that I had pounded against the door. It was red, but I doubt it was severely hurt.

"Why did you tell them you wanted to move, if you don't want too?" He must think I'm completely incoherent.

"Uh, well, I wasn't sure if I wanted to stay, but I sort of had an…epiphany," I murmured.

"Oh and what was that like?" he said while crossing his arms across his chest.

"I sort of, um…"

"You sort of what?" he sounded annoyed.

"I love you," I finally said after a short minute had passed.

I looked up at his face, which seemed expressionless. Did this mean he didn't feel the same way? Was I being rejected once again by Adam Wilson? I was truly becoming pathetic.

"Oh, well, come in." He stepped aside so I could walk past him.

Without a moment's hesitation, I entered Adam's house.

18

"So, are you sure?" Adam asked once he had offered me a drink and food. I declined both. We were now sitting in his living room; I on the couch and he across from me, sitting down.

"I don't need anything," I said.

"No, I mean are you sure you love me?" he asked, staring intently at my face.

"Yeah, I'm pretty sure," I muttered. I could feel the blush coming back.

He got up and sat next to me on the couch. "So what does this mean?"

"Well, do you love me?" I asked, not wanting to hear the answer because I was afraid of rejection, especially by this guy.

"Of course I do, you know that." He smiled with warm eyes.

"Actually, I didn't," I laughed humorlessly. He loved me? Since when? Because clearly, at my brother's funeral, he wanted no part of me.

"Oh, well I do." He was staring at his feet now.

From his profile, I could see that his eyelashes were extremely long and his jaw was even more striking.

He grabbed my hand that was sitting on my leg.

There we sat, in silence.

* * *

"I'm home!" I yelled up the stairs.

Now, came the hard part. After professing to my mom that I so badly wanted to move, now I had to explain to her that moving just wasn't an option.

My mom came galloping down the stairs. "Alright, how'd it go?" she asked with a smile.

"How did what go?" I asked, though, I already knew what she was talking about.

"Which one is it? That Chase kid, or what was it, Adam, I think?" she asked while grabbing a bottle of water out of the refrigerator.

"It's Adam. So you know what I'm going to tell you already, don't you?" I winced.

"I already am working on unpacking your things," she walked over to me and hugged me with one arm.

"Thanks mom." I kissed her cheek.

I started to run up the stairs, but then stopped. "So you aren't mad at me?"

It took a few seconds for her to answer. "We all fall in love, Scarlett."

I smiled at her and then continued to my room.

Though I had changed, I think I've changed in a better way. I'm now not sociably awkward. I now have great friends. I now know what love feels like.

As I walked into my room, I spotted the phone that was lying on my dresser.

I quickly dialed the number I wanted to become familiar with.

If this is what it felt like to be happy, then I'm not going to deny it.

The ringing ended – someone had picked up.

"Hello?" the recipient asked.

"Elaine! Guess what?" I said enthusiastically into the phone.

For the first time, I realized what I had been searching for all along – my real home.

LaVergne, TN USA
22 March 2010
176836LV00001B/20/P

9 781608 444281